CUTHBERT
Sledgehammer to Crack a Nut

#7

by

Patrick Barrett

A Wild Wolf Publication

Published by Wild Wolf Publishing in 2016
Copyright © 2016 Patrick Barrett

ISBN: 978-1-907954-56-6
Also available as an e-book

www.wildwolfpublishing.com

Chapter One

The farmhouse door slammed and dust drifted down from the beams. The cooking range coughed itself awake and growled angrily at the intrusion.

Cuthbert looked up as Percy entered. "I thought we had an agreement, Percy? Every time you lose at 'Sledgehammer' you go to your shed first, so you can slam *that* door before you come back here."

Percy snarled and thumped a bag hard onto the table top as he passed Cuthbert, stomping upstairs without another word. His dog-eared rule book was tucked firmly into his turned down welly.

Cuthbert studied the scene before him. The bag had split and brightly painted little plastic men spilled across the old farmhouse table. The figures were tangled together as if no thought had been given to chipped paint or broken limbs.

Sounds like sporadic, distant thunder echoed around the upstairs as Percy slammed his way around. He could not beat the spotty adolescents at the club, but at least he could give the house a good thrashing!

Cuthbert swept the little painted men into a bowl. Percy spent hours painting them- they were his creations. They all had fearsome weapons and grimaces and each one wore a metal painted helmet. Cuthbert also noticed for the first time they all had *red hair*. He shook his head sadly. Percy had created four hundred little Percy's.

Chapter Two

Henry held the door open for what seemed like a procession from the netherworld. Creatures with shoulder length hair and rucksacks shambled past and muttered some inaudible message of thanks for the weekend.

It had been Margery's idea to rent out the huge upper room to the war-gaming club. They arrived on a Friday night with rucksacks full of mysterious implements and disappeared until Sunday night.

Refreshments were sent up at regular intervals and all communication was achieved by secret knocks or whispered requests through the gap under the door.

The only break in the routine was when voices were raised as someone contested the referee's decision, and the usual sore loser stormed out.

Henry had this off to a fine art now; as soon as he heard the commotion, he counted to fifteen and held the door open for Percy. It was better than having the glasses rattle as it slammed behind him.

Percy paced his 'war room' and glared at the half completed models scattered across the table. His paints and brushes were stored in a pyramid of sticky leakage at one end and the finished army stood proudly at the other. Percy thumped the table and all his little men jumped obediently. Convinced his new strategy would wipe the board, he had refined his tactics until he could almost set his army to music.

Cuthbert even presented him with a book called 'Sledgehammer for Dummies' and he had accepted it gratefully without spotting the irony at all.

Percy studied that book day and night. He knew all the armies by name and colour, and he knew how to beat even the most threatening of vehicles. Nonetheless, he had been beaten by that hairy kid with the home-made 'Stamper'. Percy had never heard of a Stamper and had insisted it didn't exist.

The other gamers went into a huddle and produced a battered rule book. They also had a copy of 'Sledgehammer for Dummies' and showed him an illustration.

Percy fumed. He had only read as far as chapter three, 'How to win your first battle.' What more than that could he possibly need to know? What really hurt though was that the hairy kid made his own Stamper from an old flower pot. Percy was a gardener; he had thousands of the things!

Ronald and the Captain watched the war gamers leave. "Huh," snorted Ronald, "it's like watching the 'Miss Yeti' competition on the catwalk."

The Captain waited until Henry joined them at the table and offered, "Wouldn't last five minutes in the jungle, that lot."

Henry was accustomed to the pair of them by now. His brother Ronald had been mixed up with every murky department employing an acronym as a title, and the Captain was undefined 'ex-military'. Henry had covered trouble spots all around the globe as a reporter and as a newscaster; he saw nothing wrong with a bunch of lads staying indoors war-gaming.

Margery, his wife, thought that it was 'sweet'.

Chapter Three

Cuthbert turned as someone knocked on his door. Replacing the bowl of little men, he heaved the door open. *Percy has bent the hinges this time,* he thought.

The man at the door had no face. Actually, he was bald and regarding some papers in his hand. Looking up, he addressed Cuthbert. "Percy Plumm?" he enquired.

Cuthbert was so relieved when all the man's facial features appeared in all the right places that he simply stepped aside and let him in.

The man entered and took a seat at the table. Because Cuthbert remained silent, the man assumed he was Percy. He fanned out his sheets of paper and spoke. "The role of Grand Dragon Dropping is a very serious commitment, Mr Plumm. You will be the holder of *the power.*"

Cuthbert watched the man hold his hand out and rotate his fingers as if using the combination lock on a safe.

So far, Cuthbert had assumed he was about to be saved again. Every so often, every religion known to man would end up at his door trying to save him from something. When he was young, the Valley had cried, "The Russians are coming!" but he hadn't yet discovered what the latest threat was.

"Mr Plumm?" asked the man, slightly concerned.

"Sorry, it's just …!"

The man smiled and said quietly, "I understand, Mr Plumm. I too was speechless when I first met a *Lesser* Dragon Dropping; it is part of our journey through the Emerald wastes of Katchum."

"Oh," said Cuthbert, relieved, "as long as it's normal then."

A gasp from the stairs attracted both of the men's attention.

Percy scuttled down to stand before the man and hopped from one foot to the other. He suddenly remembered himself and opened the invisible safe.

The man at the table repeated the gesture with a suspicious look at Cuthbert.

Percy glared at Cuthbert as well, as he ushered his visitor up the stairs.

Cuthbert shrugged and walked over to where he had left Percy's plastic model figures on the hot stove.

"What does this dragon dropping look like then?" asked the Captain later in the Mandrake Arms.

Cuthbert shrugged. "Not very impressive. He was a bit like a librarian sacked for not being dynamic enough."

"Looking in the mirror, were we?" enquired Ronald nastily.

Cuthbert turned to him and said, "Be careful, he's got the power," and he opened the invisible safe.

Avril, the reporter, talking to Henry at the bar, blanched. "Where did you learn that?" she asked Cuthbert.

Cuthbert relayed the morning's events and Avril sat with them. "You have lost him," she announced dramatically. "It's a cult. I investigated it once and drove it underground."

"You mean they are in the tunnels?" barked the Captain, looking at the floor.

"A cult," grinned Ronald. "Perhaps they will shave his head and make him wear orange!"

Henry nodded solemnly. "Avril's right. I reported on them once. People get wrapped up in fantasy cultures and some of them even disappear."

Ronald shook his head. "Nope, still can't see a down-side." He was really enjoying himself.

Just then, Percy entered the bar and joined them. He sat and looked around at the shifty eyes and quaking shoulders. "What's wrong with you lot then; what's he told you?" he asked, nodding towards Cuthbert.

Avril leaned forward and patted his hand before walking away.

Ronald could simply not contain himself any longer, "Who is going to be a *little* Dragon Dropping then, Percy?" He buried his head on his arms and roared with laughter, muffling the sound with his sleeves.

Percy blushed. If the story was out, he may as well explain it, even to this lot. "If you must know," he began, but was interrupted by Ronald.

"We must, oh yes, we really must know!" and he smothered his giggles again.

Percy composed himself. "I have been approached by the lesser dragon dropping on behalf of the Great Dragon Dropping to become a student of the order of Dropping Dragons." He leaned back proudly and folded his arms.

Ronald howled with laughter. "If you don't manage that, will you just stay constipated?" He rocked so far back in his chair that he tipped over and knocked himself out.

Percy smiled smugly in the silence and nodded towards Ronald. "Yes, mate, wait until I've got some *real* power- that's just a sample."

The air of disbelief around the table seemed to suppress speech. Cuthbert hazarded, "Why Dragon *Dropping*, Percy?"

Percy watched him carefully in case his 'power' would be needed again, but then he brightened and explained. "They have this huge banner, you see. We are accepted into the order under this massive picture of Dragons flying above the clouds, but one of them is dropping to Earth, see? That's the 'Great Dragon Dropping' to watch over us and give us his power."

He beamed at his audience and Cuthbert spluttered, "Oh, Dragon *Dropping,*" in relief.

Percy scanned for traces of corrosive cynicism, but everyone was nodding. The Captain actually seemed to have nodded off. Percy announced that he had "a war to prepare for and a flower-pot to paint" and left.

The occupants of the table gave a collective groan.

Ronald gave a moan too, mostly because his conscious self poked the left side of his brain to get his body to join in and wake up.

Henry pretty much summed it all up when he began to collect glasses from the table and said "Only in the Valley" with a rueful shake of his head.

Percy stomped back to Cuthbert's farm. His 'war room' was priceless. Not only could he glue and paint there, but he could practice his skills and develop 'the power'.

He surveyed his ranks of little men and focused his concentration upon them. His blood pressure built up behind his temples and his hat quivered.

The little men stared back from above enlarged incisors and jutting jaws; they didn't seem unduly bothered.

Percy took a breath and relaxed. He sat on a chair and put his feet up on the table, dislodging a bowl. It rattled about on the floor and Percy stared in disbelief. There, right before his eyes, was an amalgam of little plastic men. The bottom of the heap was bowl-shaped and the top was an apocalyptic vision of screaming faces and clawing hands holding weapons- they had melded together in a symbolic end of the world sculpture! Percy gasped at this evidence of his fledgling power and then he smiled. Perhaps his moment had come after all.

Chapter Four

Avril told the ladies about Percy and his new obsession; gossip about one of the men was always riveting.

The Captain's wife, Elspeth, shook her head slowly. "Do you think they've brainwashed him?"

Arkle snorted, "I have a horse with more brains than Percy."

Elspeth agreed. "True! It would only take a quick rinse and a spin cycle."

Geraldine had always found Percy to be an irritating little twerp. As a museum curator and archaeologist, she took her history seriously and Percy's tales of faux ancestors could set her off in a flash. "As long as he doesn't involve us, I don't see where we need to care," she said.

Margery tutted. "Now, girls," she admonished, "he does have his uses; he kept the draught off me when the window in the bar was left open."

They all sniggered and moved on to other business. As long as it was someone *else's* business, it was fair game.

The Captain and Ronald walked aimlessly. Some days they enjoyed each other's company because they both had military backgrounds and could share war stories, even though the Captain's experiences seemed to go back to the Boer War.

They had been discussing the merits of the Zulu spear against a modern machine gun and decided it didn't have any, when they spotted Percy. He was at the base of a huge, old tree and seemed to be performing some sort of fertility dance.

The two men stood and watched as Percy grabbed a large stick and began beating the ground, before giving the actual tree a good thrashing.

The Captain coughed politely and Percy turned to glare at them.

Ronald decided that diplomacy was needed, so he asked, "What exactly is our resident twerp in wellies doing now?"

Percy, gasping for breath, panted, "*Leaves*! Gardeners *hate* leaves-nature's junk mail- *kill leaves*!" He sounded like a cartoon robot.

The Captain shuffled in embarrassment as the truth dawned. "It's not about the leaves though, is it, Percy?" he asked.

Regaining his breath, Percy asked, "Isn't it?"

Ronald listened in amazement as the Captain contributed something useful to a conversation for the first time since they had known each other. "It's the devastation of losing a battle, isn't it, old chap?" He put an arm around Percy's shoulders and steered him away from the tree.

Ronald removed the stick from Percy's hand and followed them.

The Captain muttered reassuringly, "Every General experiences that feeling, Percy." Percy looked at him gratefully as his new mentor continued. "Imagine looking over the battlefield and seeing all those brave fellows laying there. What a waste!"

Percy agreed. "Especially after all those hours spent painting them."

The Captain hesitated. "Er, well, yes, that as well, I suppose." He pressed on. "That's why Generals always leave the field after a battle, Percy; it's so they remain objective."

Ronald snorted, "It's so they don't get lynched by the survivors."

The other two ignored him and they found they were close to Percy's shed. The Captain had succeeded in cheering Percy up a bit and they agreed to have tea with him and discuss tactics.

Standing in the shed with their noses almost touching and no room to lift a cup, Ronald commented, "We can't swing a chicken in here."

Percy brightened. "Is that the first lesson?"

"Is what the first lesson?" repeated the Captain.

Percy hopped from one foot to the other. "Is it an exploding chicken?" he asked eagerly. "Does that decimate the front rank, allowing me to charge through the middle? How many chickens do I need?"

The two men lifted Percy between them and carried him outside. The claustrophobic shed seemed have an effect on all of them.

Outside, standing a reasonable distance apart, Ronald asked, "How could you live in that dump, especially with that rough blanket?"

"What rough blanket?" asked Percy. He went back and peered into the doorway, before storming down the path to them. "Typical," he snapped, "the badgers have moved in while I was away."

Chapter Five

Sitting at Cuthbert's table, Percy explained the rules to 'Sledgehammer'.

It seemed that some characters were humans, some were demons, and some were aliens. Of course, some were half-human, some were half-demons and some were aliens who were just visiting.

All these different races were at war with each other for no known reason and it wasn't entirely clear where the survivors would live after they had destroyed each other's planets. And all this was decided on the roll of a dice.

As the afternoon wore on, Percy made many notes and stuffed his instructions down his welly. He was more confident now, but felt compelled to return to the chicken throwing suggestion.

Ronald sighed and explained yet again it was just an expression.

However, the Captain pointed out that in medieval times huge catapults were used to throw dead cows over castle walls during a siege. This was early germ warfare, as the corpses would spread disease inside the castle.

This distraction ended the day and they left Percy with loads of new tactics to try. The chicken incident *should* have been forgotten.

Chapter Six

A few evenings later, Cuthbert, Henry, Ronald and the Captain were trying to play cards with no aces and only forty-two cards, when the door crashed open and dust fell from the beams.

"Percy," snapped Cuthbert, "you are supposed to slam your *shed* door. We agreed!"

Percy banged his bag onto the table and sat at the far end glaring at everyone. "The badger has locked it!" he snapped in return.

The Captain asked, "How did the battle go then, Percy?"

Percy glowered. "I lost." He scowled at each of them in turn.

It was up to Ronald to ask resignedly, "What happened this time?"

Percy took a moment and then began, "You know that tactic where my front rank advances and the two sides curl around the sides?"

Ronald and the Captain nodded enthusiastically.

"Well, I didn't use that one."

The nodding stopped.

Percy went on, "Then there was the one where I should pretend to fall back and lure them into a trap?"

The nodding resumed.

"Well, I didn't use that one either."

Ronald snarled dangerously, "Well, what *did you do?*"

"Germ warfare," said Percy proudly. "I mixed your idea with my idea and fired chickens from my catapults at the enemy."

The Captain sat back in utter disbelief. "You started the battle by firing chickens at the enemy?"

"And still lost?" added Ronald sarcastically.

Cuthbert was looking at Ronald's cards and swapping the ones he didn't need, so he kept quiet.

The Captain shook his head. "So what did the enemy do?"

Percy raised his voice. "They laughed!"

Ronald tried, "Did you explain that they were *diseased* chickens, Percy?" asked Ronald, trying to stop the laughter escaping past his teeth, but the tears still ran down his face.

Percy slumped. "They laughed even more. It's a conspiracy," he announced, before stomping off upstairs.

13

Ronald took one of the little men out of the bag and studied it.

"Do any of you get the impression that he has put his entire personality into these little chaps?" he asked, wiping his eyes.

Percy sat alone at the kitchen table.

Cuthbert had been invited to an undertakers' seminar. He hadn't actually gone, but he was strutting around telling everyone he had been invited.

Percy jumped as the door bulged inwards under a fierce pounding. He opened it to a shape with no light showing around the edges. "What do you want? Cuthbert isn't here."

Constable Beeching removed his helmet and began to squeeze from side to side as he eased his bulk into the room. "I know," he panted, "it's you I have come to see."

Percy sat cautiously. The trouble with having a colourful past was that you never knew which bit of it had just caught up with you.

The Constable placed his helmet safely on top of the cooking range and made a chair disappear beneath his bulk as he sat. "I have had complaints about disturbances, Percy."

"*Bat watching*," snapped Percy quickly.

"Bat watching?" asked the officer curiously.

"Yes," continued Percy defensively. "That's why I go out at night and lurk in the trees dressed in dark clothing."

The Constable scratched his head and said, "That's not what I meant."

Percy brightened. "That's not what I do then!"

Constable Beeching watched his prey carefully. He had pursued this character before and even had him in the cells several times. Somehow, the next morning, Percy was always gone and an 'Inspector Plumm' had always signed him out. Percy obviously had friends in high places.

The Constable produced his notebook and flipped past all the pages filled with fast food outlet phone numbers. He began by saying, "This is a new one on me, but a group of *teenagers* have complained about *you*."

Percy gazed indignantly at the officer. "Well, what were they doing in the woods at night then, eh?"

The officer countered with, "I thought you weren't in the woods?"

Percy replied, "I wasn't, but *they* must have been to have seen me."

The Constable read from his book in a ponderously official voice. "The Valley chapter of the Sledgehammer Society have accused you of causing several disturbances and an assault with a diseased chicken."

Percy gaped. "They didn't believe me when I said it was diseased."

Constable Beeching was elated; this was a confession. He had only seen those on TV when he went out of the Valley to escape the pressures of not arresting anyone. He leaned forward dangerously because the chair threatened to break. "You admit it then, Percy?"

His hand crept around his back in a vain attempt to reach the handcuffs on his belt. Then he remembered he actually kept an emergency bar of chocolate in there and gave up.

Percy narrowed his eyes. "Who accused me- that long haired one?"

Beeching shook his head. "No, the other long haired one."

Percy was aghast. "I thought he liked me!"

"That must be the third long haired one," the Constable suggested.

Percy nodded and was silent for a moment. When he spoke again, it was in a quiet, accusatory tone. "This is the fault of those dwarves."

"Dwarves?" asked the officer, scribbling in his notebook.

"Oh, yes," whispered Percy. "When they failed to assassinate the King, the whole country was plunged into chaos."

The Constable quickly counted the pages he had left in his notebook and hoped this wouldn't be a long confession. "Assassins, you say, Percy, dwarves and Kings?" He scribbled furiously.

He could *smell* promotion. Actually, he could smell his helmet melting on Cuthbert's cooking range, but having never smelled either event before, it was an easy mistake to make.

"So where do these dwarves come from then, Percy?" asked the Constable.

Percy considered this for a moment. "A dark, wooded world full of swamps, I believe."

The Constable scribbled something and then ran out of paper. He had a thought. "These dwarves aren't inside your head, are they, Percy?"

"No!"

"Well, how do they get here then?" persisted Beeching.

"The long haired one brings them in a carrier bag."

"Oh, *the long haired one*," whispered Beeching.

"Not that one," said Percy impatiently. "The other long haired one."

"Are you sure?" asked the Constable.

"Of course," insisted Percy. "The other one brings the crisps."

Chapter Six

Cuthbert had run out of people to tell about his invitation; everyone seemed to be busy. As soon as he got close to anyone, they said, "Good talking to you, Cuthbert, catch you later," and they dashed off. Cuthbert was miffed. You would have thought his success would be of interest to the Valley.

Then he saw Avril at her desk behind the big window facing onto the street. As she had her back to him, Cuthbert managed to enter her office before she could 'get busy'.

Avril stared at Cuthbert. He had insisted she write down the fact that he had been invited to a seminar of the funeral director's guild. "Did you enjoy it?" she asked politely.

"Oh, I didn't go," replied Cuthbert.

Avril tapped her pencil against her notebook. She now avoided buying the ones with the shiny spirals; she and Cuthbert had a history when it came to shiny spirals.

Cuthbert smiled fixedly at Avril as she asked, "Let me get this straight- you want me to report that our local undertaker did *not go* to a seminar of the undertakers guild?"

Cuthbert nodded. "That's right."

Avril was bemused. "Exactly why would that make front page news?"

Cuthbert could not believe he was doing this reporter's job for her. "*It's got everything,*" he exclaimed. "Local celebrity, foreign travel and up to date solutions imported into the Valley." He looked keenly at Avril and repeated, "*It's got everything.*"

She gazed back and retorted, "*It's got nothing,* Cuthbert; *you didn't go.*"

Chapter Seven

Police Constable Beeching lumbered back to his car, squeezed inside and then bumped off down the farm track. He tried hard to avoid these complicated cases, but they made a point of looking for *him*.

He had left Percy at Cuthbert's, because that's where he would find him after an escape anyway. This business about dwarves troubled him, so he scratched his head. That was another thing. He couldn't for the life of him remember where he left his helmet. He only realised it was missing when he spotted a badge just like his on Cuthbert's cooking range. Whatever Cuthbert had been cooking had run all over the front of the cooker.

Avril stared at the space emptied by Cuthbert when he stormed out in disgust, unable to accept he had described a complete non-event. She may as well fill the paper with articles about 'Piglets which hadn't been born' or 'New breakthrough in farming techniques which hadn't happened yet' or even 'Pulitzer prize winning journalist from the Valley who definitely hadn't won it yet'.

She sat alone at her desk and sobbed gently as her certificates faded quietly on the wall around her.

Cuthbert had a favourite spot where he could calm down, or even *think* if he was desperate for something to do. The old reservoir was the highest point in the Valley and it was always dry. It was also ever attended by Whistle who insisted upon fishing there.

Whistle was there now, hunched over his rod with his hood up over his head.

Cuthbert sat beside him. The hood turned slightly to acknowledge his presence, but no-one spoke.

Eventually, Cuthbert muttered his way through his imaginary troubles and Whistle cast a line quietly to not scare the non-existent fish.

Percy studied his little men. According to the Captain, it was all about tactics, but what if his men simply weren't scary enough? He rubbed his chin thoughtfully; he needed bigger axes for a start, and some vehicles.

Cuthbert's outbuildings were always a good place to start.

He took a lantern along because there was usually a body Cuthbert had forgotten to bury lurking somewhere.

After fighting through boxes of newspapers and old empty chocolate boxes, Percy found a trunk. Rusty hinges screeched in protest when he opened it and then he gasped.

These must be Cuthbert's old toys, he thought. Odd, because Cuthbert always pleaded a deprived childhood, claiming he used sticks and wool from the sheep to make a forest, and he only played at field hospitals because all his soldiers had bits missing.

Right at the bottom, he found tin-plate vehicles and old Dinky toys. This was the Holy Grail for 'scratch-built' model makers. Percy handled each one reverently and absently apologised when he nudged an embalmed body standing in the corner.

There was a compartment in the lid and this revealed the basis for Percy's revenge, Meccano! Those strange looking strips of holes surrounded by metal were perfect for fabricating war machines and transport for his men. Percy began to unload the trunk.

Cuthbert waited for Whistle's reply almost as patiently as Whistle waited for the fish that weren't there.

Eventually he risked, *"Well?"*

Whistle seemed to rouse himself.

Cuthbert suspected he had been asleep and glared at the nodding hood.

Whistle replied with, "On the one hand, Cuthbert, you are indeed a local celebrity; but on the other hand, you didn't do anything. Unfortunately, now I've run out of hands, so Whistle will have to wait and see what the future brings when the whistle blows."

The hood dropped and Cuthbert could actually hear him snoring this time.

Brushing himself down, Cuthbert stood and looked across the Valley. Why was no-one actually any use when needed, he wondered. Was it just a rumour they spread when things were good?

He headed home and entered the farm kitchen as Percy finished setting up his new finds on the table.

"Wow!" exclaimed Cuthbert. "Who gave you these?"

"You did, I suppose," replied Percy evasively.

Cuthbert snorted. "Fat chance, these are the toys I never had, look at them." He began pushing cars along the table and making embarrassing 'brumming' noises.

Percy watched him for a while and then said, "These were all in a trunk in your outbuilding, Cuthbert."

Cuthbert stopped playing. "They can't have been; I never had anything like this."

Percy took his friend to the building where he found the trunk.

The body had slithered down onto the floor and Cuthbert actually trod on it as he headed for the trunk to examine it. Stencilled on the lid was, 'Captain Horace Hoggle.' Cuthbert gasped, "He was a family legend. He sailed the South China Seas and sent back all sorts of strange souvenirs. What was he doing with these?"

Not to be outdone, Percy offered, "One of my ancestors was a seafarer too."

Cuthbert added vaguely. "He sailed a schooner with three masts."

Percy retorted, "My ancestor had four masts!"

Cuthbert remembered, "He always said he had a crew of twelve."

Percy crowed, "My ancestor had a crew of twenty, and he was seven foot tall and wore an eye patch!" He folded his arms and smirked, just as Cuthbert delivered his 'Coup-de-Grace'.

"Yes, Percy, but my ancestor *existed* outside of someone's over-fertile imagination."

Percy folded his arms tighter and humphed, "Fair enough."

They both examined the trunk again and Cuthbert leaned inside to check for a false bottom.

Percy began to intone, "These things may sort out that strange child. He really shouldn't be playing with sticks and sheep's wool. I was at sea at his age."

Cuthbert's voice echoed dully from inside the trunk. "I suppose that's a possible theory, but my dad would have given them to me." He lifted his head to find Percy holding a faded old letter. It was signed 'Horace'.

Cuthbert sat at his table surveying these toys from yesteryear. "They must have assumed it was more of his stuff and never bothered to open it," he decided.

"Always supposing that *you* were the *strange kid*, of course," said Percy mischievously. He had wound up a clockwork clown-car and it wobbled across the table with the tin clown firmly in control.

Cuthbert clicked his fingers in his unique way- it produced no sound at all- and said, "That's it!" Cuthbert ran out without another word. He even left the door open.

Percy sighed and began collecting up all the toys from the table.

Avril groaned as Cuthbert appeared in front of her desk. She had fitted a bell over the outer door to warn her and it gave a desultory 'clonk' in the background.

He came in so fast it hadn't had time to swing back.

"What is it now, Cuthbert?" she asked wearily.

Cuthbert panted, "Local celebrity finds untouched toy hoard in trunk."

Avril sighed. "If it's one of your trunks, I'm amazed you didn't find a body."

Cuthbert was appalled. "All *those* trunks are labelled." He described the hoard of collectable toys Percy unearthed and watched as she wrote everything down.

When Avril stopped writing, she looked at him warily. "I'm not sure that anyone would be interested. It seems to be a boy thing. None of my girlfriends collect their old stuff."

"Have you seen how boys play?" Cuthbert demanded. "It's a miracle if anything survives at all. These are rare memories; they must be worth a fortune."

Avril hesitated; she had an arrangement with her editor- *he* shouted and *she* listened. She rang him at home for advice and sure enough, *he shouted*! She held the phone away from her ear as her editor repeated Cuthbert's 'Boys toys' speech almost word for word. In fact there were some words in there Cuthbert didn't even know.

Editorial tension leaked out and filled the room.

Avril addressed Cuthbert. "After some serious editorial discussions and a frank exchange of views, I will accompany you and bring a photographer with me immediately," she said through clenched teeth.

The phone rattled in her hand and Avril jumped, straightening to attention immediately. She looked at Cuthbert and asked, "You didn't have a clockwork clown car amongst it all by any chance, did you?"

Cuthbert remembered Percy winding it up and nodded. "It works as well," he said.

The editorial sigh was audible in the room.

After the obligatory, "Yes, sir, of course, sir" and a very risky "You have my word, sir," she put the phone down.

Cuthbert waited, Avril sighed and admitted, "It looks as if you have really hit on something this time, Cuthbert. The editor loves the story and has been searching for a clown car for years. Apparently, his was lost after a day by the river when his brother used it as a submarine. On this basis, you will get your headline and I will get a raise. Those cars are worth a fortune now. Well done both of us."

Chapter Eight

Cuthbert beamed and waited as the photographer assembled his equipment.

Percy hadn't bothered to shut the door after Cuthbert left, so the visitors were ushered straight into the kitchen. *The table was bare!*

Cuthbert looked around frantically, before shouting upstairs, "Percy! Where is everything?"

"Up here!" came the reply.

Cuthbert beckoned and the three of them headed for the 'war room.'

They found Percy on his stool surrounded by dismantled cars, trains and aeroplanes.

A tin clown stuck on top of a pencil grinned at them as Percy stepped back with a flourish. "Just in time!" he announced.

Four pairs of eyes focused upon a stripped down tin-plate chassis wobbling across the table tipping Percy's little men out of it as it went. What was left of it was tangled between the jaws of Percy's pliers. Percy's grin froze as the focus changed to him.

Constable Beeching sat in his new patrol car thinking about the 'Percy Case.' He should have been sat at his desk, but the garage adjusted the steering wheel and driving seat and now he could not get out. It seemed to him they took an awful lot of trouble fussing around him and he was now quite suspicious.

That was the trouble with being an officer of the law; these little things get noticed.

There was no doubt in his mind that Percy was an odd little chap, but he seemed to know an awful lot about these dwarves and strange creatures. The Constable sighed; he wasn't exactly popular with his superiors. They always glared at him once they remembered who he was.

I need more information, he thought.

He fiddled with a little TV screen on the dashboard. It told him how to get to the next town, but not how to get out of the car.

Margery was outside the Mandrake Arms admiring her hanging baskets when PC Beeching pulled up in his shiny new car. He seemed to fill the whole interior and Margery was reminded of a moulded block of soap sold around Christmas.

She welcomed him politely and raised an eyebrow when he made no attempt to come inside and claim his free pie.

After lots of false starts and hesitations, the officer came to the point. "There have been allegations about hostile behaviour, Margery."

Margery smiled. "Oh, come now, Ronald has been almost civilised since we printed that lovely obituary last year."

The Constable shook his head and the car aerial wobbled. "No, not him. Those young lads who play upstairs, there are stories!" he said mysteriously.

Margery was amazed "Nonsense! They are no bother at all."

"Well, I've heard differently. I need you to keep an eye on them and report to me."

Margery bristled. It was one thing to be civil to this clomping plod, but this was too much. "I will do no such thing!" she stated.

The Constable smirked. "What about your licence, Margery?"

Margery narrowed her eyes. "What about it?"

"I can have it stopped. You wouldn't be able to make a penny without it," he crowed.

Margery was no fool; she looked him square in the eye and said, "We don't make a penny anyway. We don't charge for anything."

The officer snorted. "Of course you do, I saw you."

"No, you didn't. You have seen our customers giving to charity. They hand us the money and we send it on." Margery smiled now as she asked, "Have *you* ever paid for anything, Constable?"

Beeching spluttered, "That's different, I uphold the law, we get perks with the job."

Margery stayed silent as the officer racked his brain. His chins wobbled as he turned to face Margery again. "I saw you give change last night."

Margery thought quickly. "Oh, that poor chap didn't want to give *all* his money, so I gave him his bus fare back."

Beeching glared and snapped, "How do you pay for new stock then?"

"Oh, Constable," Margery shook her head as if it was all too obvious, "the charity gives us loads of stuff to give away, because it encourages our customers to donate even more."

The Constable got redder and redder and it was only partly because the heater blew right up his trouser leg.

He tried to say something else and Margery awaited the event with interest, but in the end he drove off without a word.

Margery stared into the distance. She could feel the air change in the Valley; something was about to happen, that was certain.

Chapter Nine

Inside the Mandrake Arms, when Margery entered, Percy was discussing tactics with Henry and the Captain; it was rumoured that he daren't go back to Cuthbert's just yet.

Margery attempted to clear the table, but was repelled by the men. Apparently, the empty glasses were bunkers, the beer mats were troops and the full glasses were *very* jealously guarded.

Ronald wandered over as Percy explained the different powers of the armies of his opposition. It all went right over Ronald's head. He had fought everything on legs in his time and recommended "getting them all paralytic on local booze before stealing their guns, bows, clubs or whatever kept them cocky."

Finding local booze which worked on little plastic men was another matter, but Ronald had solved the problem as far as he was concerned and he sat quietly.

Percy complained that he was only allowed a certain number of men in his army and he kept losing count because there was a hole in his bag.

This time the Captain came to the rescue with, "Aha! I knew a chap when I was in the camel corps; clever chap for a foreigner. It was his job to count the camels before and after the battles; he stood there for hours as they were herded past him all together. We were amazed by his dedication to the job, but eventually we discovered he only did it to sell the extra saddles without anyone noticing."

"The relevance?" prompted Henry gently.

"Oh, it was the method, you see," continued the Captain. "Handed down in the family for generations, only they knew it, so they monopolised the task for years."

"And the method was?" prompted Henry again.

The Captain gave a secretive smile and leaned forward. "The crafty blighter counted all the legs and then divided by four!"

He sat back satisfied that he had just imparted the wisdom of the ancients, but Ronald asked, "Wouldn't it have been quicker to count heads?"

Cuthbert sadly swept the remains of the tin-plate clown into the bin and seethed at the way Percy had escaped through the window.

Revenge was a contact sport and he felt denied. Even his emergency jelly-babies weren't cheering each other up, probably because they were lined up to be eaten.

Munching away reflectively, he gazed at Percy's immaculately painted armies, and then he looked at his jelly-babies, and felt a grin sneak across his face.

Chapter Ten

Cuthbert was once attacked by a bull. He was reminded of this event by the way Percy charged into his kitchen, nostrils flaring and looking around wildly.

The Captain, Cuthbert, Ronald and Henry all looked up as the door rebounded against an old football and knocked Percy back outside again. The ball had been placed there for this very purpose and they all nodded knowingly.

"That seemed to work then!" exclaimed Ronald.

Percy staggered back in rubbing his nose.

"How did the battle go then, Percy; did you do as we suggested?" asked the Captain.

Percy scowled at Cuthbert as he spoke in low menacing tones. "Oh, it went brilliantly, thank you," he spat. "I opened with a fusillade of chickens, sent my cavalry out in a pincer movement and advanced up the centre with everything else. It was a rout. I won every roll of the dice, exterminated all before me, and even the Mega-Lords of Zord ran away."

He was still glaring at Cuthbert and the assembly sensed that all was not well.

"That's all right then, isn't it, old boy?" asked the Captain, always late to pick up on a vibe.

"All right, all right?" spluttered Percy. "It would have been fantastic, except that I was disqualified."

Completely focused on Cuthbert, he emptied his bag of little men onto the table before them.

Ronald picked up one of Percy's battle hardened warriors and almost put it down again before he spotted something. "Why have all their faces melted?"

Everyone selected a figure, and Henry said, "Standard of painting has slipped a bit, Percy."

Percy slammed his fist onto the table and not only did all his little men jump obediently, all their faces fell off.

As Percy stepped forward, Cuthbert was gone.

A house full of secret passages could be a real advantage at times like this.

Hidden behind the panelling, he heard Percy wail, "I had registered my usual army and at the end someone spotted their faces and accused me of substituting a regiment of 'Melted Mud Men' to gain an advantage, so they disqualified me."

Cuthbert smirked in the dark. He spent ages cutting the faces off his jelly-babies and sticking them onto Percy's army.

They reached a truce. This always happened when one of them achieved an equal level of insult. This was referred to as 'Newton's Third Law of Notion.'

The complete set of laws reads:

Law one-Steal someone else's good idea!

Law two- Adapt it for your own purposes.

Law three- Use it for mischief.

Even so, truce or no, Cuthbert chose to still cook his own meals.

Chapter Eleven

Henry had been sent into the cellar to tap a fresh keg of ale.

This bit of theatrical description was expected from 'mine host'. In reality, he would uncouple a quick-release pipe from one thoroughly modern barrel and fit it to another one, but the customers always squared their shoulders in anticipation of the coming delight.

He had splashed half-way across the cellar when he noticed that his socks were wet; this thought suggested that his shoes must also be wet, so he stopped and looked around. The cellar was ankle deep in water.

Retracing his steps, Henry squished back upstairs and announced, "Something's leaking, chaps!"

Most of the older customers quickly checked the floor beneath their feet and looked up again with a relieved grimace.

Percy ambled across; he was rapidly becoming the Valley's resident handyman. It was a case of; if you needed a professional and there simply wasn't one, send for Percy.

His turned down wellies allowed him to penetrate further into the disaster area and he shouted bravely back up the stairs, "Stay up there, everyone, it could be dangerous."

Henry and the customers stood enthralled at the top of the stairs imagining Percy deciding which colour wire to cut as he saved the world.

Margery entered the bar to find it was empty. This was unheard of. She looked around; even Henry was missing. She began to prowl.

Henry shouted down the stairs, "How's it going, Percy?" and the others crowded around to hear the reply.

It came faintly. "Difficult ... dangerous ... supreme sacrifice ... save yourselves ..."

Henry turned to his customers and found himself staring into the eyes of his wife. "Ah, Margery," he said, "everything is under control, dear." His voice faltered slightly as he saw the hardness in her eyes and he was forced into an explanation.

Margery's eyes hardened even more and her voice took on the quality of a vampire's fingernails on the glass of a bedroom window.

"You have a leak, so you send Percy into a cellar full of best quality ale and let him convince you to leave him *alone* down there?"

Henry opened his mouth to answer, but he was almost knocked off his feet as Margery bellowed, *"Percy get out of there this minute!"*

Percy appeared at the foot of the stairs and then disappeared again. Then he climbed two steps before slipping back three. Eventually, he negotiated all the hazards by coming up sideways and leaning against the opposite wall. He then stood smiling blearily at two Margery's, neither too pleased with him.

Margery began to steer Percy towards the door, saying, "You've had more than enough for today," when she caught the sound of his wellies squelching across the floor.

Steering him towards the sink, she stated flatly, "You can empty those into the sink before you go, my lad."

With great regret, Percy hopped about removing his wellies before pouring two welly-full's of best ale down the sink. With drunken mock dignity, he clutched his wellies to his chest and made to leave.

Margery pointed him at the door and asked, "What is the problem down there anyway?"

Percy tried to focus on Margery, but she insisted upon swaying about. "The problem is, my dear," he slurred, "that you need a plumber," and he fell flat on his face.

Chapter Twelve

The Great Dragon Dropping sat on a raised podium beneath the huge tapestry showing the dragon wars of legend. The image he was named after appeared to be about to lick his balding head as it fell to earth. The Lesser Dragon Droppings were arranged on either side of him, but at a lower level.

"Let the candidate enter," announced the man in the highest chair. The doors creaked open.

About half-way down the room, Percy tripped slightly as his wellies caught each other. He stopped and moved the rule book onto the outside, to stop it happening again.

He stood before the team of men and the dramatic tapestry, and said, "Good evening, your high-ships. If this is about throwing chickens, it was only a strategy and ..."

A bang of a gavel on the table top interrupted him. "Silence, candidate, it is not your turn to speak yet."

"Sorry!" said Percy.

The lesser dropping repeated, with another bang, "Silence, candidate!"

Percy removed his hat and twiddled with it. "I was only explaining ..." he began.

Another bang. "*Silence, man!* Observe the vow of silence immediately."

Percy muttered, "I didn't know there was one."

"There is now!" snapped the Lesser Dropping.

Percy twiddled his hat silently.

The Great Dragon Dropping spoke. "We have heard about your successful battle against superior odds, brother."

Percy studied him. It seemed unlikely, because the man didn't even have red hair. "I was robbed," began Percy, before remembering the oath he hadn't taken.

The great dropping continued, "It was a test, brother. No-one can win all the time, but we also appreciate brothers who can embrace failure."

Percy brightened. "Oh well, I'm your man then. I have ancestors who have failed at almost everything ..."

The lesser dropping was banging his gavel so hard that the handle broke and hit him between the eyes and he had to be carried out of the room.

The Great Dragon Dropping was impressed. "It seems the power will be strong in you, brother. You must learn to use it only for good."

Percy's jaw dropped- had he done that to the gavel? He must have; now he *was* silent.

The man in charge spoke again. "We need to expand our activities, brother. We need men like you to organise life-size events, we need brothers of strength and imagination. Can you do it, brother?"

Percy nodded, his mind a whirl of images, most of which involved him wielding a huge sword and smiting his enemies.

The Great Dropping continued, "We also need suitable land to construct our fortifications and stage our battles, brother. Can you fulfil this role?"

Percy nodded again and a new gavel was produced and used to announce the creation of a new 'Lesser Dropping' with responsibility for '*Sledgehammer World.*' Percy was in his element; people were coming up to him and congratulating him. He was the star of the show!

After several tiny glasses of sherry, he found himself surrounded by admirers and one of them happened to say, "So, brother, tell us about some of your ancestors."

Percy shuffled, looked around and began. "According to legend, we redheads were a thrifty lot and refused to enter Noah's Ark because he wouldn't give a bulk discount for families, only couples, so we hijacked a passing albatross and reached the high ground first. For some reason, everyone else has considered the albatross to be bad luck ever since. After that, we seem to have come over with the Vikings because red hair has spread everywhere since then and, of course, everybody you talk to is a gardener."

"Were the Vikings gardeners then?" asked a brother.

"Of course they were," stated Percy proudly. "They carried those big axes to clear the vegetation and those poles with a point on to grow vegetables up."

"Broccoli spears then?" asked a bemused brother.

"Exactly," affirmed Percy.

At the far end of the hall, the Great Dragon Dropping was in discussion with his sub-ordinate. "Don't worry, brother," he was saying, "if this scruffy little twerp can get us a foothold in that secluded

Valley, we will be poised for further expansion. This could be the start of the biggest dragon dropping site of all."

His eyes shone with messianic fervour, but his second in command had been listening to Percy and wasn't sure this little chap was the key to their future at all.

Percy had just assured the other brothers that the long ships had been built that shape for transporting cucumbers from Norway, and he was now explaining that all the gold and silver they took home wasn't plunder; it was simply the monks paying for their vegetables.

Chapter Thirteen

Margery entered the cellar and approached the plumber.

From what she had seen so far, his method seemed to consist of facing each point of the compass and scratching his head.

She had left to make him a cup of tea, hoping that when she got back he would have completed the circle and actually done something.

He accepted the tea gratefully and slurped noisily.

Margery raised an eyebrow and he explained, "That's the proper way to drink tea, missus, it brings out the flavour." He tucked a thumb into his bib and braces overalls and gazed around curiously. It was his first visit to the Valley, but he had heard rumours.

"Have you always been a plumber?" asked Margery, looking for a way to ask when he intended to *start being one*.

"Oh no," replied the man, "I was called to the church, you see."

"Did they have a leak?" asked Margery.

"No, no, I was *called,*" he emphasised. "When I was a young man I wanted a bike, so I prayed and prayed but nothing happened. All my mates had a bike and I was jealous. When I asked how they got them, they told me they came from the vicar. So, obviously, he had a more direct line than me, and I went to see him. I had actually tried ringing the vicarage, but a recorded voice said, 'If you want to confess, press one. If you want to be saved press two.' And so on. I waited ages, but it never mentioned a bike, so I gave up. I had to visit the church itself. It was a calling, you see! Anyway, when I met the vicar and asked for a bike, he called the Police and I was arrested. It turned out that the first lad had stolen the vicar's bike and every time he bought a new one, someone else swiped it. He thought I was trying to short-cut the procedure."

Margery asked, "So you gave up on the priesthood then?"

The plumber slurped his tea and nodded. "Yes, but it was the thought of a pipe-line to God that made me become a plumber, you see?"

Margery nodded. "Well, it would, wouldn't it?"

The plumber gave her a frank appraisal and said, "You know, I was a bit nervous about coming here, after all the rumours about the place."

Margery smiled thinly. "Would that be the rumours about all the tradesmen who disappeared because they didn't get the job done?"

The plumber paused in mid-slurp as he looked past her smile. "Er, I'll make a start then, shall I?"

Percy walked home with a spring in his step. He was solely responsible for the creation of Sledgehammer World. It would be the theme park to end all theme parks. He would have full-sized men in costumes to play with and he could rig all the battles so that his team won. This time when he fired his chickens, he would blot out the sun.

Reaching a high point, he surveyed the Valley. Where would be the best place to site it, he wondered.

Tactically, he needed a fort each side of the Valley for the armies to meet in the middle and hammer each other. Basically he needed *the whole Valley*.

He would have a word with Cuthbert; he didn't seem to use much of it anyway.

The plumber sidled around the room clutching his tool bag. He kept his back to the wall at all times and his gaze constantly flickered to the door.

Margery was behind the bar washing a glass and all the eyes in the room followed him.

"I'll be going now," he stammered. "Can't find a thing ... no pipes ... no clue ... no charge!"

He bolted for the door and money changed hands as bets were called in. He fell over one of the Valley mafia, sending spanners and spares in all directions. He ran for his van and abandoned his tools as the rest of the mafia arrived, picked up the tools and set up a stall selling them even as he drove away.

Percy arrived at the Mandrake Arms just before all the shiny spanners changed hands around the Valley, and treated himself to one.

Joining the others at a table, he fiddled with his new adjustable spanner until he tightened it onto his thumb and had to keep it hidden under the table out of sight. He was careful not to accidentally use his power inside the crowded bar. It seemed to be growing in strength with little effort on his part.

Chapter Fourteen

Avril had been missing for a few days, meeting newspaper editors and asking about the Dropping Dragons. None of the news was good.

It appeared this was an organisation which recruited impressionable young people and involved them in fantasy war-games involving spending money on models, buildings, paints and accessories, and was quite an earner.

Some people were hooked forever, and skulls and mystic runes had been seen fitted to walking-frames.

Avril sat in her office with her back to the world thinking *at least the Valley was safe from this mob* just as Percy trundled down the street behind her pulling a hand-cart filled with axes, spears and bows.

He appeared to have a modified paint can on his head.

Henry and the Captain stood in the cellar and pondered the problem with the water. It was definitely water, so it wasn't a leaking barrel, but there were no pipes in the cellar.

Henry had thought about the tunnels, but they only flooded when it rained.

"Is it getting higher?" asked the Captain.

Henry leaned forward and poked a stick into it. "Yes, definitely. We will have to close the pub if this keeps up."

Both men fell silent at this revelation.

Percy trundled through the Valley pulling his hand cart. He whistled away to himself as he went.

Various bushes moved on each side of him as the Valley mafia monitored its territory.

Percy was really pleased with himself. His experiment with an old paint can had worked and he now owned a metal helmet. The plastic handle fitted neatly under his chin too, so it wouldn't fall off.

He didn't see anyone following him, for he was planning a mass production system to supply both armies. He was going to be rich! His mind soared on the wings of ambition and he soon imagined his men wearing burnished copper breastplates made from old hot water cylinders and carrying spears tipped with gleaming tin-foil points.

Passing an isolated cottage near the end of the village, he speeded up a bit; this was where Mister Micklewhite shot the postman. Apparently, they had been having a running battle for years, because the postman simply would not shut the man's gate. Eventually, as Mister Micklewhite explained in court, the postman left it open again and allowed the fog to creep right up to his front door, so he shot him.

Percy slowed again when he felt safe, and a hand reached out of a bush as he passed and stole an axe from the back of the cart.

The weapon disappeared into the foliage.

Henry and the Captain decided to consult Cuthbert about the water problem. Not because he had any special insight, but he had a warm kitchen and the tea was free.

Ronald joined them and they stared at the map they had all contributed to, with each of them drawing the tunnels they remembered. It was almost complete, except for the fact that none of the tunnels seemed to link up with each other. It was difficult to draw a plan view of something you had only seen from the inside in the dark.

Margery had dispatched the men, to think straight. It was difficult trying to solve a problem with men around; each had to contribute a certain length of noise, complemented by lots of nodding until one would rub his hands together and announce it was time for a drink.

If God had created Eve first, she thought, everything would have . been tidied up, ironed and filed away. He wouldn't have bothered with the men at all.

Percy reached the proposed site of Sledgehammer World and studied the terrain. He imagined a wooden stockade on each hillside facing each other. They would be made from felled timber and flags would stream out from above them.

He climbed up the hillside to check on his moat. It wasn't actually a moat yet, of course; he had dammed a stream and redirected it into a hollow where it would become a lake. He would cut a channel and let it fill his moat, genius.

Looking down into his Percy-made lake, he absently scratched his paint can helmet and wondered why the level wasn't building up. Surely a hill-side couldn't leak?

Returning to his cart, Percy rummaged around for an axe; it was time to chop down a tree. He would strike the inaugural blow. Or he would have done if he could find an axe. Kicking the cart in frustration, Percy glanced up and saw movement. He could have sworn the bush had just moved.

"Valley mafia," muttered Percy. "I should have known." Grabbing a broomstick from the cart, he charged up the hill and attacked the bush. Pieces flew everywhere and leaves fell like confetti.

Percy lunged, parried and swung until the bush was simply no more; then he stood panting with exertion.

Jasper watched from the next bush up the hill and congratulated himself. *Always pull a second bush behind you with fishing line,* he thought. *We don't want Percy getting all observant now, do we?*

Margery analysed the problem in her own way. It was obvious that the water came from outside the Mandrake Arms. It was also obvious that water flowed downhill. It was *blazingly* obvious something had changed recently and that *someone* was responsible for that change.

She had lived in the Valley for long enough to know there were two main someone's in the neighbourhood. One was Cuthbert and the other was the Devils evil twin, Percy.

It would be a simple matter to walk into Cuthbert's farm through the secret passage and confront him, but Margery knew from experience, if you took Cuthbert by surprise, two people's sanity would be on the line.

Besides, she thought, *if I creep up on Cuthbert and scream, what have you done now, I will get panic-stricken confessions going back thirty years, including every fly he ever swatted in anger.*

Hearing a commotion outside, Margery went out to investigate. The Valley mafia had set up another tool stall and Jasper was arguing with Percy.

Margery smiled fondly. Jasper was a true Valley rogue; if you wanted it, Jasper could get it. If you didn't want it, he would make sure you needed it. And if you thought you already had it, then you had probably already lost it.

He reminded her of her own dear twins. They joined the diplomatic corps and spent their time making sure everyone fought everyone else abroad, thus giving home a chance to sell weapons to all of them.

Percy glared at Jasper.

Jasper adjusted his baseball cap from 'innocent schoolboy' to 'cheeky market trader' and practised his 'artful dodger' smile. "What can I do you for, my fine feller, me lad?" he asked cheerily.

"That's my axe," snarled Percy, pointing at the table between them.

Jasper blew out his cheeks and tipped his hat back into 'Cor blimey, guv'nor, you've got me there' mode. "Can that be possible, sir?" he asked respectfully. "I appear to be in possession of it and possession or grasp is nine tenths of the law."

Percy exploded. "I don't care if grass *is* nine tenths of the floor!" he yelled. "That's my axe!"

Jasper appraised him silently and noted the flush of desperation and the sense of a furtive secret. Then there was the paint can on his head.

"Where did sir last see the axe which apparently resembled this one?" he asked silkily, moving his hat into a position where his eyes were shaded like the soul of a lawyer.

"It was, it was on my, it ..." Percy was suddenly conscious of Margery in the doorway. She always looked at him as if she was reading a script. He blustered, "It was where it was when somebody took it."

Percy didn't like being studied from two different angles; it was like those hinged mirrors where you could shave both sides of your face at once and still only do one of them.

Jasper moved in for the kill. "Would sir like to replace his missing axe with one which is remarkably similar?"

Percy glanced from Margery and back to Jasper and found himself nodding.

Jasper beamed and, turning his cap right around so that the peak was at the back and his face was a picture of innocence, he rubbed his hands together and said, "For you, my boy, a special price!"

Percy reached for his wallet, but found that one of the mafia had already got it and was counting the money into Jasper's hand. Percy clutched the axe in one hand and the empty wallet in the other and stamped off down the street muttering furiously.

Margery watched him go with narrowed eyes.

Chapter Fifteen

The women collected at the Mandrake Arms, It was the usual get together, but Margery had organised a picnic instead of being inside. Everyone contributed and shared the various baskets and flasks between them; then set off chatting away.

"Don't bother, Jasper!" snapped Margery as they passed a bush. The bush obediently took a pace backwards and waited until they were out of sight before running off for a different disguise.

Mrs Biggle had stayed behind to run the Post Office and she had promised to phone them if anything occurred.

They in turn promised to watch for a puff of white powder because she always confused her mobile with her compact.

Elspeth had always loved picnics abroad, until her husband the Captain banned her from going with them. The men had been out on the backs of elephants all day trying to hunt the big cats, without success. They fired off all their ammunition on the way back out of frustration, only to find Elspeth in a clearing feeding the tigers.

Geraldine enjoyed the escape from the museum; her place was outside amongst the ruins. If she wanted to spend the day surrounded by old dead bodies, she would rummage around in Cuthbert's outbuildings.

Arkle trudged along casually lifting baskets from everyone as she passed, until she carried the lot; it seemed to balance her, so no-one protested.

Margery steered them up onto the hillsides and they spread a nice gingham cloth out to declare the place an official picnic site.

Avril had caught them up along the way and they admired the view together.

Margery asked Geraldine if she missed the foreign excavations and Geraldine thought for a while. "I suppose I do, because we all dream of discovering that ancient city and going down in history." Her eyes took on a faraway look.

Elspeth patted her hand and offered, "There, there, dear, I'm sure we will see a bronze statue of you soon."

Geraldine answered distantly, "A donkey more like."

"Pardon, dear?" asked Margery.

Geraldine explained. "Well, the truth is that most of the great discoveries were made by donkeys."

The women could still remember when Geraldine had carried an emergency black pill in her bra, and Arkle shuffled nervously as memories came flooding back.

Geraldine saw the ripple run through the group and rushed to reassure them. "No, really! Tutankhamen's tomb was found when a donkey fell into a hole, and so was Troy. There really should be a bronze donkey somewhere."

Elspeth contributed, "That's very true. I used one once to discover the Captain. He had been on a bender with Squiffy Mortimer and was missing for days. I loaded up all my belongings ready to move home and the donkey, with all the crockery, fell over him in the back yard." She sighed. "Life could have been so different if we had kept going."

The women nodded sympathetically. They all had an 'if only I had kept going' moment at the back of their minds.

Chapter Sixteen

Cecil Carruthers was a surveyor, a man of straight lines and neat notation. He would go to any (carefully measured) lengths to finish a job, even one as strange as this.

The secrecy of this operation had been stressed from the outset and he eased his long red and white striped pole through the brambles as quietly as possible. Behind him, his apprentice crashed through the undergrowth like a three-legged wild boar in sunglasses.

Cecil tensed and waited for the youth to catch up.

When the allocations were announced, Cecil was pleased to have the chance to pass on his wisdom and work ethic to a keen young mind. However, at the end of the line had been Winston and, as the people in the line were sent in various directions, it was obvious that they were destined for each other.

Cecil appraised the young man and had been impressed by his firm's dedication to Care in the Community. This poor young man seemed to have a constant twitch and a hearing aid. His eyes were hidden by a fringe of hair and his speech seemed limited.

The manager appeared convinced Cecil was given the pick of the bunch and didn't pass on special instructions at all. Cecil wasn't married and he wasn't a father, but he was determined to become an excellent mentor. It was only after consulting with some of the secretaries that the truth dawned; he had been given *a teenager*.

The twitching was a neurological affliction caused by being wired up to a device which emitted a tinny rattle all day long. This apparently subdued all normal reactions and responses, reducing the carrier to a shambling half-life spent under hair. The only time Winston came to life was when his mobile phone erupted into a metallic voice shouting 'Incoming!' followed by the sound of an explosion.

Winston would then produce the phone with the speed of a gunslinger and proceed to send finger blurring text messages throughout the universe before slumping back into the defeated posture of one with his whole life before him.

Margery shaded her eyes and stared across at the opposite hillside. The women followed her gaze and watched as a man with a striped pole leave the tree-line cautiously, followed by someone who tripped and sent boxes and papers all over the hill-side.

"Do you see them, Jasper?" asked Margery.

"Already there!" announced a lightning damaged tree trunk as it moved away from them.

Several voices tried, "Is that why we are up here, Margery- what's going on?"

Margery kept her eyes on the two figures as she replied, "We will soon know, girls, we will soon know."

Cecil squinted through the theodolite at Winston holding the striped pole on the other side of the Valley.

He waved for his assistant to move to the left, Winston waved back. Cecil was old school and taught Winston all the hand movements, but this modern youth was only happy if he could press things and they made squawking sounds back at him.

Cecil sighed and picked up the walkie-talkie. "Can you hear me, Winston?" he asked, wincing as his assistant replied.

"Roger, full strength, come back?"

The youth was monosyllabic until hooked up to anything electronic. Then there was no stopping him.

Cecil squinted through the lens again and said, "Move left, Winston, left. *With* the pole, Winston, *pick up the pole,* Winston. No! Don't put the walkie-talkie down to pick up the pole, Winston!"

Cecil sobbed quietly as he watched Winston juggle his responsibilities across the Valley. In desperation, he dialled the young man's phone.

"Incoming!" followed by a whistling noise echoed across the Valley before Winston replied, "Go, dude!"

Cecil took a deep breath, "Winston, stand in front of that tree trunk and hold the pole upright, *please!"*

"Yo, dude!" came the reply.

Cecil looked through the lens again to make sure that things were in order and then made a notation in his book. When he looked back, the tree was off to Winston's right.

He dialled again. "Incoming" followed by an explosion echoed around the hills again.

"Winston," hissed Cecil, "you've moved, *stand in front of the tree!*"

"Yo, dude!" said Winston and Cecil watched him move.

Jotting down the time, Cecil checked the lens and gasped.

The tree was off to Winston's left now!

He had kept the line open this time and snapped, "Winston, you've moved!"

"Not me, dude, it was the tree!" said Winston.

"Oh, really," said Cecil sarcastically, "and did it tell you why it was moving, Winston?"

There was a moment's silence before his assistant replied slowly, "Not really, it just said 'cool ring-tone dude' and walked away."

Cecil took a deep breath and then wished he hadn't. Could he smell horse?

Chapter Seventeen

Percy had spent hours hammering and burnishing his paint can; now it went to a point and gleamed in the sunlight.

The crow had been watching and was impressed; now he could spot him from the air easily whenever nature called.

Percy ransacked Cuthbert's outbuildings for tools or anything useful to begin building his empire and found his Holy Grail.

The chainsaw was old and heavy, and it was impossible to tell where the metal ended and the rust began. It also ran backwards.

Percy was speechless. Why would Cuthbert own a chainsaw that ran *backwards*! Did he think he could put the trees *back up*? When he cleaned it he found foreign writing on it- perhaps the trees grew in the other direction over there?

Cecil shook his head to clear his vision. The last thing he remembered was the smell of horse and a crushing bear-hug from behind. Now he found himself sat on a tree stump with his striped pole inserted through his jacket sleeves like a scarecrow.

Off to one side stood Winston, still plugged in and swaying like a slow motion demonstration of Saint Vitus dance.

Cecil focused upon the scene before him. A group of women were gathered around some sort of ceremonial gingham cloth and *they had weapons*.

In another time and another place, he would have recognised cutlery and a picnic when he saw it, but this was the Valley and he had heard rumours.

A huge woman in tweed appeared and steered Winston closer to Cecil. The smell of horse seemed to accompany her and she removed Winston's ear-piece to get his attention.

Winston froze. The world was suddenly a scary place. He had always lived with a background sound-track like in the movies, but now he was bombarded with sounds not of his making. He stopped jigging about because his limbs refused to react to the sounds of wind and menace.

Marjorie smiled at the pair. "Now, gentlemen, what precisely are you doing here?"

Winston gaped, the woman's voice matched her lip movements and he heard what she said *without any electronic aids whatsoever.* "Cool!" he said.

"We'll find your jacket later," said Margery dismissively, and addressed the older man. "Well?"

Cecil trembled. In another time and another place it would have been a reasonable question, but this was the Valley and, again, he had heard rumours. He sensed the huge one move behind him and he quickly gabbled, "A survey, madam, just a simple survey."

Margery glanced at Winston staring around as if he had just been disconnected from his life support machine, which in fact he had. "I can see where the 'simple' bit comes in," she said, "but why the survey?"

The ground behind Cecil trembled slightly and he caved in completely. There was little dignity left with a pole shoved through one's clothing. "It's for the Sledgehammer Society; they commissioned it."

Winston said dreamily, "Sledgehammer, *cool.*"

Margery asked irritably, "Has anyone seen his jacket?" before concentrating back onto Cecil. "Who runs this 'society'?"

"The Great Dragon Dropping," stammered Cecil, feeling extremely silly saying it out loud.

Winston echoed, "Dragon Dropping, *cool.*"

Margery glared at him and Elspeth scuttled away to find the jacket and possibly save the young man's life.

Margery returned her attention to Cecil and he gulped. "No silly names, no silly titles, what's his real name?"

Cecil gulped again. The words were normal enough; the menace was in the delivery. This woman could have scared the Spanish Inquisition.

Winston stopped gazing around in awe for a moment to say, "Dragon Dropping, cool."

Margery shot to her feet, and Geraldine and Avril grabbed an arm each as Arkle moved to block her path.

Winston's random neurons suddenly clacked together and he sensed danger. "No, really, his name is Cool, Clarence Cool."

Avril's reporters' instincts came to the fore and she released Margery's arm and produced her notebook. "As in Joe Cool?" she asked incredulously.

Winston nodded. "That's his brother, the Lesser Dragon Dropping."

Avril tried, she really tried, but she could not bring herself to write 'Joe Dragon Dropping' in a serious notebook. She put her pencil away.

Geraldine took pity on Winston and plugged him back in. He was soon jigging away to the music in his mind.

Margery had been released and she studied the youth carefully. She had run the Valley mafia for years, she was used to teenagers, but this was different. They had obviously introduced a new strain.

Chapter Eighteen

Percy marched proudly into the Mandrake Arms, his helmet shining above the red mist of his hair.

The Captain had been sat drinking quietly when he turned and almost had a heart attack as his reflection stared back at him.

Percy sat with the Captain and Ronald and he beamed at Henry as he joined them.

"My equipment is almost complete," he announced.

Ronald, sensing the perfect opening, said, "Who would have thought *you* had anything missing, Percy?"

Percy ignored him and watched as everyone admired his helmet. "Are you being paid to advertise paint, Percy?" asked the Captain seriously.

Percy scowled. "I rubbed all the writing off."

"It's still on the handle, mate!" sniggered Ronald.

Henry intervened before the 'Dwarf Wars' could erupt in his bar. "You said nearly complete, Percy," he pointed out. "What else do you need?"

Percy slowly drew his eyes from Ronald and answered Henry. "Well," he said, "I've been reading books at Cuthbert's to try to get things right …"

"Never worked for Cuthbert," interrupted Ronald.

Percy ignored him and continued, "All I need now is an Ard."

Unable to resist, Ronald said, "Isn't life Ard enough for you already, Percy?"

Percy simply looked hopefully at the other two hoping for something sensible.

Henry and the Captain exchanged looks. Henry asked, "What on earth is an Ard?"

Percy shrugged, "Some sort of creature, I think," he said. "I was reading about this squire being hoisted by his pet Ard, so I'm thinking some sort of big dog?"

The Captain spluttered into his pint. "Petard, man, petard! It's a surcoat with the knight's crest on it. It was an embarrassment if the chap couldn't mount a horse and had to be 'hoisted by his own petard'."

51

Ronald roared with laughter; he could never decide which one he enjoyed humiliating the most, Cuthbert or Percy. He rocked his chair uncontrollably, fell backwards and knocked himself out yet again.

Percy looked at Ronald and smirked. His power was becoming awesome. Now, what did the Captain say, some sort of vest with a horse on it?

Henry shook his head at the thought of Ronald waking up with yet another headache. "Any chance of making Ronald one of those helmets, Percy?" he asked.

Percy replied, quick as a flash, "They don't make paint tins that big," and left the bar in triumph.

Pity Ronald hadn't been conscious to hear it.

Margery was deep in thought on the way back from the picnic as the others chatted away in front. Why did these two brothers think they could build some kind of theme park in the Valley?

Cuthbert owned most of it, mostly by default. When a long- lost relative died and he handled the funeral there was often a small parcel of land on a hillside somewhere. The rest of the family usually said, "Give it to Cuthbert, he'll know what to do with it."

Truth be told, he barely knew what to do with the body let alone the land.

Margery knew these things because she had kept a close eye for years and the Valley mafia didn't miss much.

Cuthbert was like a cork bobbing about in a bowl of water, he went wherever the waves took him and if you told him he wasn't a cork, he would sink.

She couldn't see Cuthbert in this scheme somehow. It had to be someone in contact with this Sledgehammer crowd. She pictured the three long-haired players who used the upstairs room at the pub- they were hardly dynamic and certainly weren't stupid enough to cross her. Who could it be?

"Percy!" cried Elspeth, and Avril echoed with "Percy!"

Good grief, thought Margery, *are my thoughts that transparent?*

Percy looked up as the two women called out to him; he had been putting the wheel back on his hand-cart, but it was too heavy with the chainsaw on it. They had just stopped him from using his power to levitate it; he hadn't seen them approaching and his secret would have been out.

"Having trouble, Percy?" Avril asked.

Percy decided to keep his secret identity secret, which made sense when you considered why it was referred to as a secret identity.

He sat on the cart as they all gathered round to look. "Nothing I can't fix, ladies," he beamed. "I'll have it sorted soon." Percy paused; he seemed to be rising above them all. He was looking down at them. He almost panicked. His power was getting stronger- would they notice?

The women gave him a cheery wave and went on their way.

Margery studied him closely as she passed. Percy plus chainsaw equalled suspicious, she thought, and planned to send out her mafia minions to watch him.

Percy didn't notice the look; he found himself upon his cart with the wheel refitted simply by using the power. He felt himself grow stronger and pulled the cart behind him with new confidence.

Avril turned to Arkle and asked, "Didn't Percy even thank you for fixing his wheel?"

Arkle shook her head. "I don't think he even noticed."

Avril was disgusted. "I've a good mind to go back and give him a piece of my mind."

"You'll have no trouble catching him," Arkle smirked. "I didn't put the nut on the axle; it should be off again right about now."

Percy stared at the cart. He clenched his fists and concentrated like mad, the veins on his neck stood out and his helmet suddenly felt very tight. The wheel lay there stubbornly and the cart refused to rise.

The crow swooped across the Valley, rolling slowly onto his back and warming himself against the sun.

Amongst the many design faults affecting a crow was the thin stomach feathers. All the top ones were wonderful, thick and waterproof, but underneath had been an economy job, and the wind-chill factor had to be felt to be believed.

Completing his 'barrel roll' the crow lowered his flaps and focused on the scene below. The 'scruffy one' seemed to be in trouble and the crow was compelled to follow the code of crows everywhere. Whenever a human seemed to be in trouble, a crow was duty-bound to sit nearby and gloat; there might always be a meal in it.

Percy allowed himself to exhale before his helmet exploded. He glared at the crow and tipped his head to one side to show that he wasn't in the mood for black humour.

The crow obediently cocked its head the same way.

Percy cocked his head the other way and the crow followed suit. *It's the power,* thought Percy. With a brain as small as a crow's, he could probably take it over completely.

Stepping towards the bird, Percy held both arms out from his side and slowly flapped them.

The crow, startled, took an involuntary step backwards and had to flap his own wings to regain his balance.

Percy smirked and thought, *if I can control the birds of the air, I can send squadrons of vultures against my enemies. I can look out over the Valley and track Cuthbert from above.*

He quickly scrapped the latter thought. The most exciting event in Cuthbert's life was when he found a new hair on his chin and then promptly forgot where he had seen it.

The crow was watching him closely and it was important not to scare it away, so he turned slowly and concentrated upon the wheel.

Holding his breath again and clenching his fists, he felt warmth spread down his cheek and into his shoulder- the power was building up!

The crow flew overhead and admired his aim before returning to his aerial patrol.

The scruffy one was fun, but the rookery would be awaiting the tales of his exploits. He flapped away leisurely.

Chapter Nineteen

Cuthbert had received a letter. After a knock on the door, this was the next most unsettling thing he could imagine.

It lay there, mysterious and secretive. The envelope had a return address on the back and Cuthbert recognised the name of his solicitors, Grumble and Grimble. They had been the family solicitors for generations, even before Cuthbert's family had anything worth soliciting.

Cuthbert nudged it along the table and studied the stamp. It depicted someone he had never heard of, doing something he didn't recognise, and just where the explanation was printed in tiny lettering someone had stamped a smudgy post-mark.

So much for fame, thought Cuthbert.

The door burst open and the Captain, Ronald and Henry marched in. Henry made straight for the kettle and the Captain spotted the letter.

"Letter, eh, Cuthbert?" he barked. "Got one of those myself once and I then spent the next thirty years in the forces because of it. Didn't get another until I came out again. That one was from my mother asking where I'd been."

Henry banged two cups onto the table and fetched more for Cuthbert and Ronald. They all sat and stared at the envelope.

"It's considered quite normal to actually open it and see what it says, you know, Cuthbert," began Henry, still smarting over the argument he seemed to have lost with the Captain.

Cuthbert picked up the vibe and used it as a delaying tactic. "What was it about this time?" he asked.

The Captain airily waved a hand and replied, "Ronald doesn't think that a padre should bless the troops before battle or some such nonsense."

.Henry glared at him. "*Both* sides have someone doing the same thing," he snapped. "If there is only one God, what's the point?"

The Captain shook his head knowingly. "Depends on the padre, old boy. Ours was really canny; he always went to the top of the nearest hill and sat alone before a battle. Then he would come down and give a rousing pre-battle speech to inspire the troops."

Henry raised an eyebrow. "Did he go up there to pray for guidance?"

The Captain sipped his tea and replied, "Not really. He always took a telescope and counted the enemy guns. If they had loads of the things he would come back down and tell us to go off sick."

Ronald sneered, "I bet he never went into battle with you!"

The Captain agreed. "No, never, but I told you he was canny."

Ronald wasn't convinced. "Some of the battles I was in would have gone down in history had they been legal. We faced massed charges from hordes of painted warriors and always stood our ground." He sat back and raised his cup for a drink.

"Did they have *big* sticks?" asked Henry sarcastically.

Ronald sprayed tea across the table and spluttered, "They were *sharp* ones!"

"The letter?" prompted Henry.

Cuthbert stared at it again. He was much better at imagining the horrors lurking inside, than he was actually reading about them.

Ronald leaned over and snatched the letter. With a practised flick of the wrist, he held onto the envelope and skimmed the letter across the table to Cuthbert.

The others stared at him.

Ronald shrugged. "Centrifugal force," he explained. "You can't leave traces when you've opened the mail of a cabinet minister." He pressed the flap back down and for all anyone knew, the letter was still inside.

Henry looked at his brother admiringly. "Please say that I can write your autobiography, Ronald?"

Ronald gave a regretful shrug. "You could, but then I would have to kill you."

Henry was even more impressed. "Code of honour?"

"No," replied Ronald. "I don't like sharing royalties."

Attention gradually shifted back to Cuthbert looking at the open letter as if an ancient Egyptian had written to him in hieroglyphs. He handed the paper to Henry without a word.

Henry scanned the writing and asked, "Did you know about this?"

Cuthbert shook his head.

Henry looked around the table and announced, "Apparently, gentlemen, Cuthbert has donated most of the Valley to some chap who likes to be called 'The Great Dragon Dropping'."

Chapter Twenty

Percy had arrived at the spot at last. His power was having an off-day. He had carried the chainsaw all the way up the hill and then gone back for the one-wheeled cart. Then he fetched the other wheel so that no-one would witness his embarrassment.

A nearby bush sniggered.

Percy planted his feet firmly apart and pulled the string to start the chainsaw. It spluttered, it coughed and it stopped. He tried again, and again. After several attempts, Percy turned his back on the thing and scowled out across the Valley, muttering to himself.

By this time, the bush was shaking uncontrollably and Jasper emerged to lend a hand. Creeping across the ground, he reached forward and turned the petrol switch to 'on', before retreating to his hiding place.

Percy, feeling fully psyched-up, turned and approached the chainsaw. Grabbing it masterfully with both hands, he gave it a final threatening stare; then he pulled the string.

Jasper watched in awe.

Percy disappeared in a cloud of blue smoke and the one wheeled cart was reduced to matchwood in seconds. Percy emerged from the smoke and seemed to judder in all directions at once, the chainsaw held out in front of him like a divining rod. When it climbed, he chopped a branch, and when it dipped, he carved a furrow.

Jasper wondered why anyone would go to school and miss out on things like this. Then he saw Percy coming straight at him and he fled.

In the midst of the spinning column of smoke, Percy saw the bush run away and assumed his power had linked up with his gardening instincts and shooed it away to preserve it.

The meeting in the Mandrake Arms produced a shocked silence as everyone took in the news that they may soon be homeless.

The only people who wouldn't suffer were the already homeless and witless, but Percy wasn't here anyway.

It was one thing to own the building, but if someone else owned the roads leading to it, there could be problems.

Once again, the only people not affected would be those who didn't have a road leading to their homes. Percy's name appeared as if by magic again.

After a quick analysis of who would actually *not* suffer from all this, it became apparent that Percy (the only one not here) had nothing to worry about.

Margery remembered seeing him several times heading for the hills with tools in a cart. She passed this on to the rest of them and they were pondering this when Jasper spoke.

Everyone jumped and Ronald 'went tactical' under the table.

They had all been aware of the huge pot plant in the corner, of course, but no-one knew that Jasper had been inside it.

He told them about Percy's forays into the hills in more detail and added the chainsaw massacre to show an escalation in the activity in that neck of the woods. Suspicious glances were exchanged.

Cuthbert adopted his neutral poker face due to a complete lack of intuition and a dearth of expressive facial muscles.

Percy beamed at his creation with pride; he had cleared a patch of ground on the hillside and already built a stockade facing across the Valley. He had a commanding view, but had to be careful not to fall into the moat. He hadn't intended to dig a moat yet, but the chainsaw got away.

"Are you sure this is the place?" whispered Henry.

Jasper nodded. "There is a big room over the top and that's where they meet."

Henry, Ronald, Cuthbert and the Captain looked around.

The narrow staircase led upwards between 'Madame Fifi's' dog grooming parlour on one side and a martial arts studio on the other.

The Captain barged in front and began to climb the stairs; these upstarts weren't getting his house.

The others hesitated as they heard the Captain's voice from somewhere above them.

"Come on, sonny, out of the way like a good lad … argh!"

Ronald moved to one side as the Captain rolled between them and out into the street. A young lad in a white outfit with a black belt walked past them brushing dust from his hands as he went.

"Did I remember to say, 'go past the martial arts studio'?" asked Jasper hopefully.

The group of men stood outside a large, solid door and read the inscription. 'Abandon hope all ye who enter here (closed Wednesday afternoons).'

"Where have I read that before?" asked Cuthbert nervously.

Henry answered vaguely as he looked around. "Dante's Inferno. It's inscribed above the gates of hell."

"Do *they* close on Wednesdays as well?" asked Ronald.

Chapter Twenty-One

Margery listened to Elspeth twittering away as she baked.

The men had been dispatched to investigate this Sledgehammer business, but something bothered her. Elspeth merrily talked to the ingredients and apologised to them when she had to attack them with a whisk.

"Now, now," she said, "you are not the correct flour for the job, now are you?" Putting the packet back and removing another, she said, "That's better, good results don't come from bad ingredients, now do they?"

Margery sat up straight; that was it! That was what bothered her; she had sent the *men* to deal with it!

Henry tried the door handle- it turned.

Ronald pushed him away. "Careful," he whispered. "Open it slowly and it might squeak, we have to go in fast and low. When I throw it open, we charge in and bomb-burst in separate directions, got it?"

The others nodded.

After a whispered "One-two-three, go!" they burst through the door and into the meeting room.

After a brief glimpse of a dramatic tapestry showing dragons and things, they fell.

Margery and Geraldine sat having tea with Madame Fifi at the back of the grooming parlour when the room at the front of the shop exploded into chaos.

Screams, howls, yelps, and then the dogs started to make a noise as well.

The women rushed into the room to find assorted Valley men-folk being savaged by an unlikely pack of poodles and Yorkshire terriers, some still in curlers.

After extricating the gallant band of adventurers, Margery explained that the room upstairs had a spot of dry rot and the door had been left open to allow the workmen access to continue renewing the floorboards.

"What sort of twit would run into a strange room in the first place?" asked an indignant Madam Fifi, eyeing the line-up in disgust.

The men shuffled in embarrassment and muttered about stealth and tactics, but Margery marched them outside and explained how simple it was to just drop in for a cup of tea and ask a straightforward question.

Once they were around the corner they all conferred.

Margery had discovered that the two men who ran the Sledgehammer club were Clarence and Joe Cool. They also owned a comic book shop and a shop supplying little plastic men for the Sledgehammer game.

"According to Madam Fifi," continued Margery, "they have obtained a huge piece of land and they are developing a Sledgehammer theme park where members can dress up and play a full-size version of the game, costumes, castles and everything." She looked at the men around her and pretended to bow to their greater knowledge of organised violence when she asked, "What sort of land would that require?"

Henry said, "That would take up a lot of room."

Ronald supplied, "Needs to be somewhere isolated; there's nothing worse than feeling silly when you're all dressed up."

The Captain rubbed his chin. "Ideally you would need two hillsides facing each other so that you can fling missiles across the gap and then meet in the middle to do battle."

Cuthbert decided that it was his turn and said, "We're safe enough then, there's nothing like that around here."

All eyes turned to Cuthbert and he felt the warm glow of taking part in a real conversation at last.

Margery hissed, "Two hillsides with a gap in the middle, Cuthbert- does that sound remotely like a *valley* to you?"

"Oh," said Cuthbert.

Chapter Twenty-Two

Percy patrolled his ramparts, his helmet gleaming and a large wooden club in his hand.

When the sun caught his helmet, it also lit up the mass of unruly red hair escaping from underneath it; aficionados of the Icelandic saga's and legends would have shivered. They would know a Troll when they saw one.

The moat glittered below him and Percy smiled, the water had been escaping through a crack in the floor of his trench, so he had dug another channel and filled his moat instead of it all leaking away. *Let the Valley mafia get past this lot,* he thought.

Just below him, a bush finished washing its socks and wrung them out in the moat. Watching Percy was so boring that Jasper had been reduced to housework.

The brothers Cool stood back and admired their handiwork.

The table-top model of the Valley was impressive. They made tons of papier-mâché to form the hills and stuffed them with women's tights from washing lines all over the area. That had been a tricky one as housewives were notoriously touchy about things like that.

Each hill-side had a fort made from ice-lolly sticks and several little plastic men stood guard to give an impression of scale.

The surveyor had done well, although he seemed puzzled by the complimentary membership card to the 'Sledgehammer Society'. His strange young assistant had appreciated it though. He always addressed them respectfully by their surnames, most things were accepted with a "wow, cool!"

Avril returned to the Valley at last, her research complete. The hectic pace of the town had worn her out. All that rushing, shouting and computer-key clacking. School hadn't been like that in her day.

She had used her contacts to investigate the Sledgehammer Society and now she addressed the assembly before her.

"The Cool brothers have tried all this before and they are determined to get their hands on a piece of land as cheaply as possible. Then, they gradually enslave the local youths with time wasting games full of unpronounceable names and logic-defying rules. The games can only be played with authorised little plastic men and authentic scenery. If they need more money, the Cool brothers produce the same army in a different colour and charge even more." She paused. "The good news is that no-one has been stupid enough to let them buy any land around here, so far."

The response was more muted than Avril expected and then she read the letter handed to her by Margery. "Oh," she said.

Marvin Middlewick had achieved his aim; his monument to the fallen colleagues of the Local Authority set in marble in Cuthbert's cemetery had made him a legend in his own time. No-one sent him any work and no-one dared to upset him, in case he left their name off the monument in future.

The knock on his door was completely unexpected; he had the crossword to finish before anyone dared to bring him a cup of tea. "Enter," he said imperiously.

Marvin was the Council Liaison Officer Supervising Excavation and Digging. This acronym (C.L.O.S.E.D.) was displayed on his door and his desk and was largely responsible for him never being disturbed.

The door opened and Margery stepped into his office. "Still not really closed, I see?" she said with a wide smile.

Marvin blushed. He had developed a soft spot for Margery during his dealings with the Valley. In an attempt at gallantry, he replied, "Never closed to problems concerning you, my dear."

"Good," said Margery, flinging the door wide and admitting everyone else who had accompanied her.

Marvin looked up at the sea of faces surrounding him in his own office and gulped.

Every face from the Valley carried its own nightmare memory for Marvin. If a pillow fell over his face in the night, he woke up screaming thinking that Cuthbert had decided to bury him.

Margery announced she had invited the drains inspector and his road gang to join them and Marvin had a quick panic attack at the thought of the combined odour of their drains and his fear, all in this little office.

Margery anticipated this and the road gang had assembled outside. A window was opened and the drains inspector, Swivelling Simon, Buster and One Lung Louie waved to everyone from outside.

Marvin was trapped.

He listened reluctantly as Margery outlined the problem and gradually he began to pay attention. Excavations, digging, all without supervision. This attacked the very fabric of his existence. He sat up straight and then straighter still when Margery mentioned the brothers Cool.

Marvin had been to school with the Cool brothers. They were boring even by Local Authority standards; the class would contribute their lunch money to a fund and pay the brothers to ask the teacher long, monotonous questions. When the poor man fell asleep, the class would disappear into the corridors clutching pieces of paper disguised as urgent messages for a member of staff. A football was hidden behind the bike sheds.

The road gang listened intently; life had been rather monotonous lately. "See one drain and you've seen them all," as the drains inspector would say.

The others would nod wisely because they hadn't yet seen them all, so they weren't sure if it was true.

They wandered back to their office. It still didn't have the ambience of the old shed, but it was getting there.

"This sounds like a job for the 'A' team," said Buster proudly.

"Shouldn't that be the 'D' team?" asked One Lung Louie.

"Why 'D' team?" asked Buster.

"'D' for drains," pointed out Louie. "'A' team tackles arson attacks, 'B' team tackles 'balls stuck up trees', 'C' team is for 'conflagrations', so we must be 'D' team."

Swivelling Simon nudged Buster as they walked along, "That's the Fire Brigade lad, he's getting mixed up; we're Local Authority so it's, 'A' team asks for overtime, 'B' team invents extra work and 'C' team clocks everybody off four hours after the others have left."

Buster scratched his head. "So there's no 'D' team then?"

Louie answered with, "You can have de team if you want de team, but de drains inspector thinks he runs de team!"

Louie and Swivelling Simon linked arms and staggered off together howling with laughter as Buster continued to scratch his head.

The drains inspector tried to concentrate. *Another foray into the Valley, eh,* he thought. *We must take everything we can think of and then all the things we forgot as well.*

Percy marched along the wooden ramparts and then paused as he spotted a crowd forming on the path through the Valley. They could be enemy troops massing for an attack or local villagers asking for sanctuary in his fort.

He was happier with crowds than he was with small groups. Two men travelling together always put him on edge- they either tried to convert you or arrest you.

Percy mentally checked his provisions. The moat was fed by clean spring water and he had plenty of food. Before leaving Cuthbert's he had taken everything edible and made it into sandwiches; he could hold out here for months.

The crowd had assembled below his walls. On the opposite side of his moat he could see all the people he knew from the Valley and, a good way behind, he could see the blue flashing light on Constable Beeching's police car where it was stuck in the mud.

Percy congratulated his power; it must have turned the road soft to keep the law at bay. If the officer tried to walk he would sink even further than the car.

Cuthbert moved to the front of the crowd and shouted, "Percy! We need to talk."

"Who goes there?" responded Percy in his best military fashion.

Margery stepped forward. "Percy, we don't have time to list everyone. Just take my word for it that everyone here wants to throttle you, but we will listen to your preposterous explanation before we do it."

Many heads nodded in agreement. Margery had missed her calling in diplomacy.

Percy banged his club on the top of the palisade and warned, "Don't come any closer! This place is impregnable and I can survive for weeks here."

"You tell them, mate!" said Jasper leaning on the wooden wall beside Percy. "Even *you* must have *some* human rights."

Percy looked around in confusion and spluttered, "How did you get here? This place is impregnable."

Jasper looked at him pityingly. "Not if you are sitting in a bush while some twit builds it around you."

Percy looked around wildly; the Valley mafia didn't ride alone. "Where are the rest of you?"

Jasper pointed vaguely across the wooden fort and replied, "Over there, eating your sandwiches."

The crowd was getting restless; there were murmurs of "burn him out" and "starve him out!"

Ronald suggested, "Lock him in, then burn him out!"

Percy glared; it was time for his 'eve of battle' speech. "Fellow travellers on this blood-soaked way," he began, "some of us will not be here to see the dawn ..."

If he had been listening he would have heard Jasper quietly counting "one-two-three" just before they pitched Percy over the top of the wall.

Landing on his helmet and red- hair shock absorber, he simply bounced before staggering around in a circle and falling into the moat.

The crowd dragged him out and Percy was surrounded by glaring eyes and pointing fingers. Everybody seemed to take a turn at explaining what he had done and why he should be ashamed of himself and indeed, what he should *do* with himself.

Percy raised both hands and the noise died down. "All right," he said, "you may have a point, but my ancestors were risk takers and they came from all over ..."

Ronald shouted, "Rip him to bits and we can chuck *him* all over the place!"

As the noise increased, Percy began to think he may have gone too far this time. Raising his hands again, he shouted, "I can show you the plans if you like!"

The murmur died down as Percy rummaged in his welly and produced a soggy brochure.

Keen hands took it from him and Percy made a run for it.

The crown shouted, "This is a seed catalogue!"

Hearing that, Percy accelerated, dodging between a forest of legs until Arkle hoisted him up and held him three feet above the ground with his little legs still pumping furiously.

"Oh, look," cried Margery, "he's been hoisted by his own pet Ard!"

Chapter Twenty-Three

Marvin addressed the road gang as they stood outside his office. He paced about inside whilst his team tried to catch everything he said through the gap in the window.

"There are rampant planning anomalies here," he said.

The drains inspector repeated, "They are planting anemones here."

"Where?" asked Buster.

"Shush," said Louie.

"We may have to tear things down again," continued Marvin.

"They are turning brown again," translated the drains inspector.

"Not very good at it, are they?" asked Louie.

"Shush," said Simon.

"We must put an end to it all!" said Marvin.

"It's by a bend in the wall," said the drains inspector.

"What is?" asked Buster.

"Shush," said Louie *and* Simon.

Marvin finished with, "We must weed out this iniquity!"

The drains inspector scratched his head. "He wants us to weed it before tea."

"Weed what?" asked Buster.

"The anemones," snapped Louie.

"But where are they?" asked Buster plaintively.

"By the bend in the wall, stupid!" they all cried at once.

The drains inspector was confused, this sounded like gardening, not drain clearing. Perhaps they should ask that Percy chap, he might know something.

Chapter Twenty-Four

The 'trial' was conducted in Cuthbert's kitchen, Percy sat at one end of the long table and his accusers sat down the sides. At the head of the table was Cuthbert, mainly because it was *his* table.

Other former friends lined the walls and Percy was the focus of all the attention.

He remembered long ago when he had started further education and a headmaster peered down at him and asked, "Is that sand on your shoes, boy?"

Percy had looked down at his turned down wellies and said, "Er, everything *but* sand, I would have thought."

The man had snarled, "No, boy, it *is* sand, fresh from the intellectual desert of the secondary schools and neither you nor it have any place here."

Percy hadn't thrived there, and neither had the window boxes when he had done with them.

He looked around the angry faces, adopted a look of pure pathos and said, "When I was first orphaned ..."

Ronald snarled, "We don't want to know!"

Percy tried, "One of my ancestors ..."

Several people roared, "We definitely don't want to know!"

The cooking range contentedly belched smoke in the hope of a human sacrifice.

Percy tried again. "The first time I discovered that the hospital had mixed the names up and I was actually my lost twin brother ..." His eyes flickered around desperately looking for a grain of sympathy and his shoulders slumped when he found none. "All right, all right," he said, "I wanted to be a 'Great Dragon Dropping' one day, so I sold them the Valley to stage full scale Sledgehammer battles."

A gasp went around the table and Henry asked, "How could you?"

Ronald asked, "How much?"

Henry insisted, "No, really, how could you, *you don't own it!"*

Percy shuffled uncomfortably and replied, "I gave them some old deeds I found in Cuthbert's secret cupboard."

Cuthbert awoke from his reverie and asked, "Which one is that?"

Percy muttered, "The one behind the grandfather clock."

Cuthbert shook his head. "I didn't know about that one."

Ronald observed, "It doesn't really matter- apparently it's someone else's secret cupboard now."

Cuthbert spluttered, "You have sold everything? Is it legal?" He looked around wildly.

The majority opinion was a shrug, but Percy muttered, "Jasper said that 'grass is nine tenths of the floor', so that makes it legal."

Margery glared at Jasper, who offered a puzzled look in return. "Does that *sound* like me?" he asked.

Everyone agreed that it sounded far more like Percy and Ronald asked again, "How much did you get for it?"

Percy shuffled again and started counting on his fingers. "Well," he calculated, "they let me have the trees for the stockade at no cost, they waived the site rent for the spot where I built it and they gave me an axe."

The silence was absolute until Cuthbert hissed, "He gave it away; he gave away the Valley!"

As everyone converged on the spot where Percy had been, Percy slid off his chair and scuttled under the table, escaping through the door and into the night.

Most of the Valley folk had slunk back to their homes to make little red haired troll dolls and stick pins in them.

Margery stroked the back of her husband's hand and said, "Henry, if no money changed hands, it can't be legal, can it?"

Henry brightened and looked around.

Cuthbert, Ronald, the Captain and Avril all nodded eagerly.

It sounded right enough.

"Good thinking," said Jasper from behind the aspidistra.

"Will you stop doing that, please, Jasper," asked Margery.

Jasper took a seat. "Sorry, force of habit."

They began to plot a method of retrieving the deeds.

Chapter Twenty-Five

Percy was hungry. The Valley mafia had eaten all his sandwiches and he couldn't get back out of his fort, because although there had been a rope strategically hanging from a tree to let him climb in and out, it wasn't there anymore and it had tasted awful too.

He had long since thrashed the leaves off any bushes looking for mafia spies and boiled the leaves to make tea. He had also tried eating bark taken from his log fort; it had been chewy and it cured his headache, but it wasn't the same as a meal.

Percy wasn't a food snob at all; he would eat anything with eyes as long as it didn't wink at him.

He glanced up at the sky; the crow was circling lazily above.

Percy's mouth watered. How could he attract the bird close enough?

He had to become crow-bait!

The crow dipped one wing as he saw movement below. The sun reflected from the scruffy one's helmet as he staggered about before falling flat on his back staring upwards with an axe in his hand.

Gently gliding across the sky, the crow lost altitude for a better view. He had been watching the scruffy one build his nest; it was certainly stronger than the crow's humble abode, but at least he could fly out of his when he wanted to.

The crow landed on top of the palisade. The scruffy one looked as if he had starved to death, which was odd because the crow could see any amount of tasty treats. There were worms, flies, slugs and caterpillars; it was like finding the keys to a bug-market.

These humans were their own worst enemies, he thought. One minute they were cooking over open fires and the next they wrapped everything up so well that the time taken opening all the wrapping constituted a diet.

He hopped from the palisade to the raised walkway feasting as he went. The scruffy one hadn't moved for some time. Perhaps he was asleep? Humans seemed to need a lot of 'down-time' compared to a crow. He had seen them leaning against things at all times of the day making strange wood-cutting sounds to warn off predators. He had often thought that the dopey one was dead, but when something has no expression it can be hard to tell.

The crow hopped onto Percy's chest and stared hard at the face beneath the polished paint can.

He cocked his head from side to side, but the sight didn't improve at all. Just to make sure, he gave Percy a sharp peck right between the eyes.

Percy's eyes flew open and the axe swung as the crow grappled with the other hand around its neck. They rolled over and over desperately trying to be the first one to eat the other. The ground opened up and they fell!

Waking up in a tunnel was not something the crow had practised. He shook his head and slowly identified the clonks and clanks of Percy's helmet rebounding off things in the dark.

The sounds were moving away from him, so he shuffled to his feet and stretched his wings experimentally.

He had always been aware of the design faults of his species and now he discovered another one. How does a completely black bird check itself for damage in the dark? He stared hard, but he couldn't see a wing in front of him. He began to hop forwards and the ground began to rise. What had been in front of him was under him and he fell flat on his back.

Turning, he tried again in the opposite direction- the same thing happened.

Eventually, he realised that two directions hurt and the other two didn't, so he hopped along in the dark.

Sometimes, he forgot where he was and took off, only to meet pain coming the other way again when he hit the roof.

His friend the magpie had once stolen a bright shiny cup given to a professor for discovering worm-holes in space.

Could this be a worm-hole leading to another dimension?

Hopping along, the crow imagined a world where crows wore the badges and gave the orders. A world where humans mined bird seed all day long and cuckoos were forced to bring up their own young.

Then another thought crept silently through the dark- what if this *was* a *worm*-hole?

The garden variety worm- the crow had pulled enough of them out of holes to recognise the shape of the hole, but his feathers broke into a sweat at the size of this one.

Visions of a world where worms pulled crows out of their nests clamoured for his attention and the thought of one of his past breakfasts hurtling along in the dark towards him gave wing assisted speed to his twiggy little legs.

He couldn't see a way out, neither could he see a way in; in fact, he couldn't see the point of his own beak. Especially, against a worm this size!

Chapter Twenty-Six

Henry had reported from wars all over the world and the Captain had narrowly avoided fighting in wars all everywhere. Ronald was *responsible* for an awful lot of wars world over and Cuthbert knew a dead body when he found it in his outbuilding.

With these qualifications, they considered themselves the ideal team to tackle the 'Great Dragon Dropping' and his sledgehammer hordes.

Ronald still had some 'tactical suits', which were basically overalls smothered in pockets shaped for various accessories and weaponry.

Cuthbert was thrilled to find a pocket that held his chocolate bar until Ronald swapped it for a walkie-talkie.

They were ready, faces blacked and pockets full.

Ronald said, "Right, this is it. I will bring up the rear, one of you lead the way."

Henry looked confused. "I don't know where it was; I was following the Captain."

The Captain frowned. "I was following Cuthbert."

Cuthbert reclaimed his chocolate and broke it into squares and distributed them around his overalls. He looked up and said, "I was following someone else as well."

"Well, who was it?" asked Ronald.

Cuthbert shrugged. "I don't know. I only recognise bodies from in front."

Henry groaned; the 'dream team' was already a nightmare! "We had better find Jasper!" he said.

"Only a matter of time," muttered the plant in the corner.

The Valley women called a meeting and Elspeth had suggested they call round to the brothers Cool with a bouquet of flowers and a bottle of wine, do some dusting and washing-up for them and ask for the deeds back.

Arkle smashed her fist onto the top of the pub table buckling its cast iron legs in the process. "I say we kick down the door, grab them by the throat and shake them until they give us the deeds- who is with me?"

The other Valley women looked hopefully at Margery to calm the situation. She addressed Elspeth first. "Lovely idea, dear, but you cannot go around cleaning things for single men. I believe there is legislation regarding that." She then turned carefully to Arkle and asked, "And you, dear, do you remember the big house on the hill where you and Geraldine spent your holidays?"

Arkle calmed visibly and glanced at Geraldine, who automatically reached for her pillbox.

Avril suggested writing an expose of the situation, but it was generally thought rather an embarrassment that one of them had given the Valley away to two strangers.

Elspeth paused from her knitting and said, "In fairness, he did get an axe for it."

Margery answered with, "Yes, dear, then he lost it and had to buy it back from Jasper. It actually cost Percy money to give the Valley away."

Chapter Twenty-Seven

Percy stumbled along the tunnel banging his helmet on the curved roof whenever he strayed from the middle. He couldn't see the crow to eat it and he couldn't see his way out either. Now he knew what a really *black* mood was.

He stopped and listened carefully, and heard clunking sounds. Hearing them earlier, he assumed it was his helmet striking the roof. There seemed to be a slight glow up ahead as well, and a rustling noise coming towards him.

The crow approached the glow from the other direction and they were converging on the same point.

Percy and the crow spotted each other at the same time in the faint light and an unspoken truce was declared when the crow hopped onto his shoulder and Percy stroked its feathers.

Shared terror can sometimes be a short-cut to friendship.

Madam Fifi was shampooing a poodle when a figure dressed all in black slid through her door, held its finger to its lips and stared up at the ceiling. The floorboards had been replaced and the hole repaired.

The short, dark stranger waved and slid back outside.

Madam Fifi sighed; no wonder she preferred dogs. You always knew what they were doing and which end they were doing it from.

Men were a complete mystery to her.

Ronald joined the others at the foot of the stairs, gave a thumbs-up and led the way upwards.

His assault team followed nervously. With various hand signals and a quick jab to get Cuthbert's attention, Ronald threw open the door.

The team burst into the room and fanned out.

At the far end, behind a long table and beneath the dragon tapestry sat the brothers Cool. The surname was well deserved as they showed no surprise at all, even when Ronald strode forward to confront them and fell through the floor.

76

Floorboards had been removed further on as the work progressed. Chaos ensued below and a wisp of pink-dyed dog hair floated upwards into the room.

The rest of the team skirted the hole and approached the table. Clarence Cool, the Great Dragon Dropping, raised an eyebrow in mute interrogation.

Henry stepped forward. "This is about this Sledgehammer business."

"Would you like to join?" asked Clarence calmly.

"No!" shouted Cuthbert. "I want my Valley back!"

A second eyebrow raised itself to join the first. "Your Valley?"

Cuthbert stepped up beside Henry. "I am Cuthbert and I hold the deeds to the Valley."

Joe Cool, the lesser Dragon Dropping, sniggered, "That's not exactly accurate, you know. Your hands appear to be empty and *we* seem to hold the deeds. Besides, the Cuthbert we dealt with looked nothing like you. Equally appalling, I'll grant you, but no similarity at all."

Cuthbert exploded. "He is *not* Cuthbert; he just thinks he's Cuthbert. He also thinks he is a gardener and he thinks he is related to Napoleon!"

Clarence stroked his chin. "You friend certainly does a lot of thinking, doesn't he?"

"No," muttered Henry, "and that's why we are in this mess."

Clarence gave a negligent wave of his hand. "The matter is settled and everything is in hand. Building work has begun and the theme park is on schedule." He offered, "We could keep some of you on, of course, as character actors and guides." His eyes danced with amusement at the thought, but Henry was ready for him.

"Do you have planning permission?" he asked silkily.

The brothers lost control for a split second and exchanged glances.

Henry turned to his companions and raised his voice. "Marvin Middlewick, step forward and do your duty, please!"

No-one moved. All his companions looked alike in their overalls and blacked out faces.

"Marvin?" tried Henry again. "Did anyone invite Marvin?"

The brothers Cool gave a sigh of relief.

Chapter Twenty-Eight

Percy and the crow leaned around a corner and focused as many eyes as possible on the scene. This generally meant three because of the shape of the crow's head and the fact that his beak banged against Percy's helmet if he leant too far across.

"Cor!" said Percy.

"Caw!" said the crow.

The scene resembled a candle-lit mining scene from the American Wild West. Tree trunks supported the roof and steel rails ran down the middle of the roadway. Over by the far wall, two men were tapping away at the rock wall. They didn't hear Percy creeping closer, because they were intent upon their work.

Suddenly, the crow flapped its wings to keep his balance and the men looked around.

The screams only added to the effect of Percy in a metal helmet and glowing red hair accompanied by a huge black crow with its wings fully extended, their shadows leaping threateningly in the candle-light.

The men fled.

The martial arts instructor glanced out of his window and spotted the group of black-clad men on the pavement below. This man knew his business; he was Sensei at this Dojo and he had seen all the films Bruce Lee ever made. He knew trouble when he saw it. He turned to address his class of ten year olds. "Gentlemen, prepare to defend yourselves," he announced gravely and bowed to them.

The class bowed in return and headed for the stairs.

The Sensei stared at the scene below him; the Ninjas were warming up ready for the attack. One of them practised ballistic kicks to prepare himself for combat, and the instructor sighed.

He had trained all his life for this moment, but somehow the pavement outside a poodle parlour didn't compare with a dramatic flight of steps inside the Forbidden City

He followed his class.

Cuthbert was livid; blood was pounding into parts of his brain on stand-by since birth. He took another kick at the empty crisp packet and it simply flounced away again. He tried to stamp on it and it back-flipped to one side.

"Save your energy, Cuthbert," growled Ronald. "You might need it for something else."

"Yeah, like what?" snarled Cuthbert, at his most dangerous.

Ronald nodded towards something behind Cuthbert and said, "That bunch of kids in their pyjamas, for a start."

Madam Fifi thought she had seen it all, but as she tended to the wounded, she shook her head as she witnessed cuts, bruises, abrasions and blood from Cuthbert's nose bleed caused by unexpected activity.

It was a wonder none of the younger lads were hurt as well.

The adults flinched as a lad wearing a black belt entered.

He gave a mocking bow and announced, "The Sensei says that I should pay respect to our defeated enemy." He then sneered and added, "I don't know why, it was like attacking a woman carrying a wet handkerchief." He then struck a pose and uttered his battle cry before leaving and slamming the door.

Ronald muttered, "He will never know how close he came."

Henry looked at him through a swollen eye and said, "With bruises like this I'm glad he *didn't* come any closer."

Cuthbert studied his own blood in amazement. His father always warned him that "violence was a messy business." He always assumed the mess would be on someone else.

Chapter Twenty-Nine

The crow tapped the wall with his beak experimentally. *Those men had really been concentrating,* he thought, *but if this is what passes for music with humans, they can keep it.*

Percy sifted through chips of stone at the foot of the wall and saw something glitter. It was just a speck in a piece of rock and it only caught the light at the right angle, but ... "Gold," whispered Percy reverently.

The crow cocked his head from side to side. *And what precisely would you do with that,* he thought. *You can't eat it, so why expend energy finding it?*

He hopped down from Percy's shoulder; he had been in this situation before. His mate, the magpie obsessed with shiny stuff, spent all his working days looking for open windows and bringing things back with him, but to what purpose? In the end, he daren't leave home in case someone stole the stuff only *he* wanted and the sheer weight made the bottom fall out of his nest.

That's where hoarding got you. Whoever coined the phrase 'nest egg' certainly wasn't a crow. Of course, an expression like 'the bottom fell out of the market' was pure avian wisdom.

Percy fondled the piece of rock. Sweat broke out on his forehead, but it *was* hot in here and he *was* wearing a steel helmet. By rationalising it, he managed to ignore the first signs of gold-fever.

He looked around. The crow was a witness, but he was not going to talk any time soon. The two who escaped, would have to be dealt with, unless ... they might have a stash somewhere.

Percy stroked his chin and tucked the rock in his welly.

The crow recognised the signs- the sweating brow, the shifty eye movements, the flick of the wrist as the nugget went into hiding. By the time it came out of Percy's welly, it would either be refined or rotted away completely.

He watched as Percy considered his options. He went from totally inadequate to mass-murderer in seconds, just because a rock winked at him. The secret would be safe with the crow, of course; he was no stool-pigeon.

The two men clung together in terror, whatever the apparition was, it was coming this way. They decided that the only way to placate the 'Troll God of the Mines' was to bow and scrape a lot and mutter gibberish until it went away.

They prostrated themselves facing the mine entrance and duly muttered sweet nothings until they heard the clomping footsteps stop before them.

Risking a quick glance, one of them said, "Here, he's not *that* big."

The other one risked a look and added, "That looks like a crow."

Then they asked in unison; "Is that a paint can?"

Jasper had 'become one' with a hanging basket when the ruckus started and he was the only one not limping on the way home.

The others tried to put a positive spin on the events ready for when they met Margery. They had decided upon "the room was full of dragon droppings and we had to bravely fight our way out to protect Jasper."

When Margery met them at the door of the Mandrake Arms and said, "I've just had a call from Madam Fifi," they simply slunk past her.

"Don't I know you?" asked one of the miners. They sat opposite one another at the mine entrance and each one watched the other carefully. "I saw you watching for UFO's when I first came here."

"You've been here *that* long?" asked Percy. "I never saw you."

The man looked at his feet. "Well, I've been underground since then."

Percy looked at the other miner. "What about you?"

"Oh, I was the postman," he explained. "Delivered letters to the Valley for years, in rain, shine, chaos and confusion."

"Chaos and confusion?" asked Percy.

The man looked at him carefully and asked, "Ever met a chap called Cuthbert?"

The ex-postman began to relax a bit and explained that over the years he had carried several letters for the gold-mine. Intrigued, he had asked about it in the Valley, but everyone was evasive. Some wouldn't even talk about it at all. One day, he had taken 'Embalmers Weekly' to Cuthbert's and, after knocking loudly, heard someone call, "Out here, in the outbuilding!"

The postman had been pleased to find someone who actually spoke and worked his way through rooms full of jars of chemicals, then rooms full of coffins and finally a room full of bodies. Determined to ask someone about the gold-mine, he persevered until he found Cuthbert in the labyrinth.

Unfortunately, by the time he had found him, Cuthbert had sewn his own lips together whilst trying to thread a needle held between his teeth.

Eventually, the postman had hit upon a plan and began asking for 'the old mine' instead of the gold-mine. It didn't set alarm bells ringing and eventually someone told him where it was. After moving in and beginning to dig, he met his fellow miner camping in the woods nearby ever since the UFO's had failed to appear. They had been at it ever since.

Statistically, the miners were not strangers to the Valley, but they had spent an awful lot of time *under it,* with only each other for company, so they could be forgiven when one of them asked, "What's your story then, Percy?"

Percy shuffled …

Chapter Thirty

Margery addressed the meeting. The women were keen to hear actions talking louder than words and listened carefully. "Well," began Margery, "we have sent out the hunter-gatherers to protect us and restore the rights to our own homes. As usual, they have come back empty-handed and empty-headed. It's our turn, girls. There are only two Cool brothers and if they think *their* dragon is powerful, they've seen nothing yet."

A huge mound of tweed stirred at the end of the table and Arkle asked, "Want me to seduce them, Margery?"

Margery smiled. "All in good time, dear; let's see what the others come up with first, shall we?"

Looks of sheer panic crossed the faces of the women present. They were used to Margery allotting tasks and sending them on their way, but this was going to take effort.

"Suggestions, please, Geraldine," snapped Margery.

Geraldine looked around. Her comrades' eyes glittered with sympathy and desperation; it would be their turn soon. She straightened in her chair and spoke. "Well," she said carefully, "I do know a member of the solicitors firm 'Bogus, Sharp and Shifty'."

The others waited and Margery had to prompt, "That's nice, dear, will it help?"

Geraldine sighed. "When we visited Madam Fifi, I looked at the letters stacked in the hallway. Several were for the Cool brothers from their solicitors, Bogus, Sharp and Shifty. I know one of the partners."

The two miners were beginning to wonder if the lack of oxygen underground had affected them. Percy had reached the stage in his family tree where his ancestor had opened an 'oil-mine'. The miners challenged this description, but Percy pointed out that oil came from underground and someone had to fetch it, so what other system would work? Then he changed the subject, whilst the last thought still raged inside their heads.

The crow knew it wasn't oxygen deprivation at all; it was Percy overload.

The postman had quite enjoyed his new life as a miner. He missed the fresh air and pirouetting on ice with his heavy mail-bag, but the rewards would be much greater in this job. He mentioned to Percy he might settle in the Valley when they found the mother lode, but Percy pointed out that things had changed whilst he had been underground.

The postman had mentioned buying Mandrake Hall.

"Burnt down," said Percy.

Building a house overlooking the lake- "Concreted over," supplied Percy.

The postman tried, "I could buy the land where Mandrake Hall stood and build there then."

"It's a cinema now," said Percy.

The postman was taken aback; these dreams had kept him tapping away at a rock wall for years in the hope of becoming a landowner. He became bullish. "I'll buy the whole flaming Valley then and put everything back."

Percy shook his head. "Too late, it's a theme park now."

As the postman (miner) lapsed into depressed silence, the other one spoke up. "We might not have enough to spend anything anyway."

Percy was immediately alert. "Why not?"

The man replied, "Our stream dried up and we haven't been able to wash the ore for ages, it's piling up and we can't pan for nuggets without water."

"I've got plenty of water!" bragged Percy, sensing a way to become a partner in this enterprise. "My moat is full!"

Both miners gave him a glassy stare. "Water? Where did that come from?"

Percy puffed out his chest and ignored the sight of the crow putting his head under his wing. "I diverted a stream further up the hill and dug a trench." He beamed at his audience, waiting to bask in the praise he was convinced was coming his way. What was actually coming his way was a pair of shovel-wielding gold diggers bent on revenge.

Chapter Thirty-One

Margery had spoken privately to Geraldine after the meeting; she had been interested to hear which solicitor her friend had in mind at the firm of Bogus, Sharp and Shifty.

"Is it the bogus one, the sharp one or the shifty one?" she asked playfully.

Geraldine thought for a moment before replying, "That covers all three of them," she said. "Actually, I'm never sure which one of them is which until I see them. We all qualified around about the same time and the celebrations were a bit blurred."

Percy backed up against the gold-face wall and the miners advanced on him with deadly intent. Percy could almost hear the last clang of the shovel striking 'A-flat miner' as they finished him off.

Inspiration dawned. "Just a minute, chaps," he babbled. "I've got an idea; I know where the rest of the water went."

Three men and a crow stared into the hole. They could see a crack in the stream bed and water was still disappearing back into the earth. The miners watched closely as Percy told them about the flooding in the cellar of the Mandrake Arms.

"I must have broken into an old tunnel when I dug the trench," he explained. "If we take the ore into the tunnel, we can wash it where the stream runs the fastest and keep it out of sight."

The two miners exchanged glances. After years underground together, they pretty much knew what the other one was thinking.

"Okay," said one of them, "but if this is a trick, the crow gets it!"

"Sounds fair," agreed Percy cheerily. The crow gave them all a black look.

Chapter Thirty-Two

Cuthbert was seething. For once, he was alone at his farmhouse table. He had been a successful, but slightly careless undertaker, a not very successful farmer and a slap-dash theatre producer. Now, all these almost-careers were in jeopardy and he could end up homeless.

He fumed in his corner and the cooking range churned in the other one. They eyed each other warily.

Cuthbert drummed his fingers on the table top. The cooking range had many moods. It could be friendly, warm and welcoming or malevolent and threatening. *Ha! A cooker with a range of disguises,* he thought. The drumming fingers paused. "That's it," muttered Cuthbert. Disguise!

It was his job to make a corpse look presentable for its final journey. Of course, some ended up with make-up schemes they wouldn't be seen dead in. The actors he prepared sometimes made the stage look like a mausoleum if he got his palettes mixed up; the standard of acting didn't help either.

He wandered off to one of his outhouses and started opening boxes.

The old man hobbled into the Post Office, his gnarled hands gripping a blackthorn walking stick. His beard was unkempt and his clothes shabby, his voice wavered as he asked for a book of stamps.

"Sore throat is it, Cuthbert?" asked Mrs Biggle. "There's a bottle of linctus here somewhere." When she turned from rummaging on the shelves, the shop was empty.

Cuthbert grumbled all the way home before he kicked the outhouse door open and started again.

Percy and the miners stood in the tunnel and held their candles aloft. Part of the roof had fallen in at this point and dammed the flow of water. Cracks in the brickwork on one side showed where the water had overflowed into the cellar of the Mandrake Arms, light seeped back out in retaliation.

"See," said Percy, "if we clear the blockage and get the water running again we can wash the ore and store it down here, right under everyone's feet."

As the miners exchanged glances, Percy elaborated, "I could offer to work from inside to repair the wall and bring supplies in for you, maybe the odd pint or two, eh?"

The miners brightened. Everyone shook hands or wings or whatever wasn't holding a candle and they went their separate ways.

Percy and the crow came out of the tunnel into the sunlight. The crow hopped onto his shoulder and tapped on his helmet. Looking in the direction of the tapping, Percy narrowed his eyes.

The man swaggering towards them wore a kilt and a bonnet and swung a knobbly stick as he came closer.

The stranger touched his stick to his bonnet in greeting as Percy said, "Nice knees, Cuthbert."

The stranger formerly known as Cuthbert fumed all the way home again and kicked the outhouse door once more, before dragging out more boxes.

Chapter Thirty-Three

Marjorie had been surprised when Percy walked into the bar; and not just because of the crow on his shoulder. He had been out of sight for a while ever since the village folk started building a gallows for him, but like most village projects, they ran out of funds and enthusiasm. Elspeth suspended a nice hanging basket from it in the end.

Percy explained his plan to 'make up for all the things he had done lately'.

This would entail a complete refurbishment of the village just from the things Margery could think of right now. In the end, she accepted his offer to repair the cracks in the cellar brickwork and stop the water coming in.

Later that day, she went down into the cellar and he was hard at work with a shovel pushing water back through a hole in the wall.

Margery scratched her head. She hadn't seen him bring tools in with him and crows don't have big pockets. She ostentatiously checked the barrels and counted the bottles before going back up to visit Avril at the newspaper office.

Crossing the road, Margery smiled at a nun coming the other way. "Sound of Music this year is it, Cuthbert?" she asked as they passed each other.

The nun spluttered something and stamped off.

Avril looked up hopefully as Margery entered; she had an edition of the local paper to write. "Anything happening out there, Margery?"

Margery thought for a moment before replying, "Not really, dear. The Captain and Henry are missing, Ronald is writing his obituary in case he has to disappear again, Cuthbert is cross-dressing and Percy is shovelling water."

Avril put down her pen in disgust. "Why didn't I get a job somewhere interesting?" she wailed.

Cuthbert picked himself up and scowled at the outhouse door. You could only kick it so many times before it kicked back.

He removed the nun's outfit before it became a habit and pondered his next move.

The building where the Great Dragon Dropping operated also contained a poodle parlour and a martial arts studio. Cuthbert rubbed his chin and eyed a winding sheet and several yards of black funeral ribbon.

The Sensei watched his pupils carefully as they manoeuvred around each other before unleashing a blistering display of kicks and punches punctuated by adrenaline fuelled yells.

The door to the Dojo opened and a man entered. He was dressed for the mats and he wore a black belt. It was always an honour to greet a fellow black belt and the Sensei bowed in appreciation. The man politely bowed back.

The class responded well to the stranger; they threw themselves and each other into a demonstration on his behalf, but the man seemed preoccupied.

Cuthbert sat at the edge of the mat and tried to listen for noises from upstairs. If this lot would stop yelling, he might be able to hear whether the Great Dragon Dropping was in residence or not.

The pupils before him eventually stood gasping from exertion and saw him staring at the ceiling.

"The stranger does not seem impressed," said a voice. "Perhaps he would like to join us?"

Cuthbert staggered back along his farm track, his white outfit trailing in tatters around him and the black ribbon around his neck.

Henry and the Captain came the other way and the Captain said, "Oh! Good one, Cuthbert, return of the mummy, eh? Well done!"

Cuthbert went looking for the door.

Percy sat on an upturned barrel and offered the miners a drink.

"Won't that Margery find out?" asked one of them.

Percy shook his head. "Last time I was down here, I rigged the compressor to the biggest barrel. We can just keep pumping air in."

The miners licked their lips; gold-fever wasn't much fun without something to cool it off.

They both accepted a drink and gulped noisily.

Henry and the Captain returned to the Mandrake Arms and joined Ronald at the bar.

Ronald proudly showed them his new obituary. He always had one prepared in case his past caught up with him and he had to disappear again.

The Captain perused the paper, his eyebrows climbing faster than a spitfire. "How did you not win a Victoria cross, Ronald?" he asked incredulously.

Ronald snatched the sheet of paper back and snapped, "That's the nature of 'Secret Operatives Designated Secret'."

"SODS?" asked Henry, suppressing a smile.

Ronald glared at his brother. Multiple concussions over many years were known to have an effect on a sense of humour. He opened his mouth to retort, but the music was getting louder by the minute and now he couldn't hear himself speak.

"Margery!" he shouted. "Can you turn the radio down please?"

Margery entered the front door just in time to ask, "What radio?"

They all listened. If it wasn't a radio, then somebody's choir was about to be sacked.

Margery put a hand up to her mouth. "Percy!" she whispered.

Henry stared at his wife. "You mean that you left Percy in a cellar full of beer barrels and bottles unsupervised, dear?" He was enjoying this immensely.

Margery raced for the cellar steps closely followed by the men. They were faced by a scene from a Bacchanalian festival.

Percy sat astride a barrel trying to escape from the Apaches and the two miners were shaking bottles and firing corks at him, all roaring lyrics at the top of their voices in three different keys at once.

The sight of Margery and her posse brought the proceedings to a halt and the three miscreants tumbled into the hole to escape into the tunnel.

Margery charged forward and pulled the compressor pipe from the largest barrel. This released the compressed air and the barrel shot off, punching another hole in the tunnel wall and taking most of the bottle racks with it. Margery put her head into one of the holes and screamed "*Percy!*" at the top of her lungs. The sound travelled through every tunnel at once and came out of exits that no-one knew about.

The men had the sense to keep very silent indeed, except for the Captain who muttered, "Was that the postman? No wonder this month's 'Military Modelling for Absolute Numbskulls' hasn't come." He then looked down and said, "Oh look. Margery, the water's gone."

Chapter Thirty-Three

Cuthbert made several attempts to imitate a poodle, but the thought of electric clippers gnawed at him and he gave up.

He threw all the coloured nylon scraps in the outhouse bin and glared at the door. The glare didn't work, for the knocking continued. "What is it with doors?" he muttered. "We put them up and shut them to keep people out and they just make a noise until we open them again."

He yanked the door open and Percy fell in *backwards*.

Two more men stood outside trying to plait themselves together in an attempt to stand upright.

Cuthbert dragged Percy over the threshold, making his helmet clonk on the floor slabs; then herded the two miners into the same spare room and latched the door *from the outside*.

Whistling to himself, Cuthbert crossed the farmyard and went to bed. It wasn't the first time he had laid three bodies out on the same night. Not that the Valley specialised in disasters, of course; it was simply that sometimes he got behind and they just accumulated.

Percy stirred as the miners began work. He had to admire them for determination, but did they *have* to keep banging?

Opening one eye, he gradually adjusted the focus until he made out the still forms of his friends slumped in a corner with someone else who didn't look at all well.

No-one was moving, but the banging continued. Eventually Percy decided it was his pulse banging inside his helmet and went looking for breakfast.

Cuthbert had unlatched the door and he glanced up as Percy entered and negotiated the furniture. His eyes were slits as he tried to filter out all unnecessary images heading for his brain.

Standing by the cupboard, Percy peered at the empty shelves and demanded, "Where's the food?"

Cuthbert finished his fried breakfast and replied, "Apparently someone made it all into sandwiches and gave the Valley mafia a picnic. Besides, I thought you were on a liquid diet now?"

Percy eyed Cuthbert's smeared plate suspiciously. "Where can I get some food then?" he asked plaintively.

Cuthbert pretended to think. "Well, I suppose a gardener could always grow his own- do we know anybody?" His suppressed grin was having an incendiary effect on Percy.

Percy cocked his head to one side; it seemed to help the crow and surely enough an idea rattled forth.

"The Post Office," he announced. "Mrs Biggle will have something," and he made his way to the door.

Cuthbert warned him, "Oh, Mrs Biggle will have *something* all right. The odds are good, but the goods are odd."

Percy was in no state to translate that one and left.

On the way into the village, Percy began to feel a bit brighter and gave a little skip which caused the rock in his welly to pop out without him noticing it, but a nearby bush saw it and moved in.

Avril sat in her office staring down the street. She saw Percy appear and then she turned to answer her mobile phone.

She had set the ring-tone to the happiest jingle she could find, but it never influenced the calls she received.

More deaths and funny shaped vegetables were on the card for next week's paper. Avril sighed and adopted a professionally pitched voice in anticipation.

Behind her at the end of the road, Percy heard a rustling and turned just as the bush scooped up his rock. He leaped into action to retrieve it.

Avril frowned as a young lad entered her office and put his finger to his lips as she concentrated on writing down the details of Mr Pickles and his amazing dog, who apparently barked precisely when it wanted to. Mr Pickles thought this was astounding and wanted to share the news with the whole Valley.

The young lad gazed over her shoulder in wonder as a scruffy little chap in a shiny helmet attacked a bush in the middle of the road. He coughed to attract Avril's attention, but she waved impatiently for him to be quiet and asked Mr Pickles to repeat something.

The lad watched fascinated as leaves and wellies flew in all directions. His jaw dropped when another bush appeared and joined in.

93

The little chap was doing all right until a lightning damaged tree-trunk appeared and waded in as well.

The young lad was a trainee reporter and had heard of 'robberies in the shrubbery' but never 'robberies *by* the shrubbery' unless of course the robbery occurred *near* some shrubbery, in which case it would be *nearby* the shrubbery.

Good grief, he thought, *there really was more to this job than met the eye.*

Avril was finishing her phone conversation and easing Mr Pickles into the idea that it may not actually be the headline next week, when the lad saw one of the bushes jam both of Percy's feet into one welly and chuck him over a wall. The tree trunk and the bushes dispersed and a gust of wind cleared the leaves.

Glancing behind her at the empty street, Avril snapped, "What on earth are you gawping at? You'll never be a reporter if you don't show more awareness, lad," and she dismissed him.

Percy struggled free from his welly and checked his possessions; the only thing missing was the glittering rock he found in the mine.

He stamped around looking for his other welly and muttered dire threats against Jasper and the Valley mafia. Of course, he made sure that none of the bushes heard him.

Mrs Biggle looked up as Percy entered. He might have looked a little 'knocked about' after his encounter, but it was hard to tell.

Percy saw that Mrs Biggle was talking to a stranger, so he approached and introduced himself. There was always a chance that the chap was looking for Ronald, and Percy could settle some old scores.

He shook the man's hand and asked, "Who are *you* then?"

The man hesitated and looked closely at Percy before replying, "P ... P ... P..."

Percy interrupted, "Oh, I know this one. Public Personnel Person."

The man gazed at him and said, "P ... P ... P..."

Percy jumped up and down. "Pope's Personal Poet," he tried.

Mrs Biggle hit Percy with the fly swatter and said, "He's the postman, he's got a stammer, you fool."

Percy rubbed his head and complained, "Well, how was I supposed to know?"

Mrs Biggle said, "Didn't the big bag of letters and the bike tip you off?"

"Oh," said Percy.

Chapter Thirty-Four

The pile of shopping burst into Cuthbert's kitchen, all stacked above Percy's wellies. The whole stack tumbled onto the table to reveal a grinning gardener still in his Sledgehammer helmet.

Cuthbert randomly examined the ingredients for the next feast and concluded that kippers and custard with mint sauce would be on the menu.

Mrs Biggle seemed to stock up at some warehouse of last resort.

Percy busied himself making a doorstep sandwich firing questions at Cuthbert all the time he worked, licking his lips as the concoction came together.

"What exactly did those scrolls look like?" he asked.

Cuthbert paused from thinking about all the things he was thinking of putting off until tomorrow, and replied, "It's years since I've seen them and I didn't even know where they were kept, but every scroll I've ever seen looks about the same. Crinkly old paper rolled up and covered in spindly writing. A deed like that would be full of 'Wherefores and who so what's and in pursuance of'. Then there would be a wax seal on the bottom; very important that."

Percy paused as if he was taking it all in and stepped back to admire his 'skyscraper sandwich'. "Okeydokey," he said. "Call a meeting for this evening and I will unveil the plan."

"What plan?" asked Cuthbert reasonably.

Percy balanced his creation on a plate and went wobbling past. "*The* plan."

"Have you made a model?" asked Cuthbert excitedly.

"What for?" asked Percy.

"So there's something to unveil, of course!" supplied Cuthbert.

Percy peered around his sandwich. "I haven't finished the plan yet, Cuthbert. It's a pre-plan in the pre-planning stage, waiting to move from preliminary to actuality. It is an invisible, imaginary concept, awaiting birth as an actual tangible asset, okay?"

Cuthbert thought for a moment. "Not a model then?" he asked.

Percy cleared a work space in his model room and proudly stood his sandwich to one side.

He laid out a sheet of clean white paper and smeared it with salad cream, before screwing it up into a ball to get some authentic creases and then rolled it into a tube. He then spent hours covering the paper in spidery handwriting and adding thicker strokes here and there to resemble italics.

The plan was then to gently bake it in the oven at 'quite a bit Fahrenheit' and roll it back up while it stiffened.

The finishing touch would be the wax seal. Percy frowned in concentration.

The kitchen cabinet gathered with absolutely no enthusiasm at all. It was gradually being seen as a lost cause.

The Valley was gone and they would be reduced to the role of cartoon characters greeting visitors to Sledgehammer World.

Henry and the Captain passed mugs of tea down the table to the others and a solemn murmur filled the room.

Ronald's idea involving napalm seemed about the best bet at the moment.

Percy appeared at the bend in the stairs and came down with something tucked under his arm.

Everyone turned to look and Cuthbert shouted "Ta-da!" because he was determined to have an unveiling.

Percy stood for a moment at the end of the table and then he rolled out his masterpiece.

It crackled, it sprang back into a roll if you didn't hold it flat and it looked absolutely authentic.

Everyone gathered round and admired Percy's handiwork and he basked in the praise.

"You see," he explained, "we substitute this for the deed they possess and everything goes back to normal, well, normal for the Valley anyway."

Everyone was impressed, even Geraldine, who was quite an expert in such matters. She knew that the content was gibberish, but first glance was all that mattered. She patted Percy's arm and everyone joined in the congratulations as Percy beamed.

Ronald's cynicism refused to be cowed and it forced him to have a look for himself. "Is that a slug?" he asked.

"Where?" yelped Percy; thinking that a gardener's deadly enemy had at last penetrated his defences.

"There, at the bottom of the scroll," said Ronald, pointing.

"That's not a slug," sneered Percy. "It's a wax seal."

Percy sulked; slugs had blighted his life ever since he decided to pretend he was a gardener.

He had spent hours out on 'slug-patrol.' His garden had a ring of salt around it and there were little pots of beer strategically placed for the slugs to fall into and die happy.

One afternoon, he still remembered, he spent hours lying in wait for one persistent slime-ball.

He sat in the bushes peering through his telescopic sight tracking \ silver trails across the paths looking for the culprit. Suddenly, there it was, black and shiny, antennae questing above it as it moved in to devour anything on a stalk.

Percy centred the cross-hairs and breathed in; then he let out half a breath to steady his aim and … threw the brick.

It bounced off the path harmlessly, miles away from its target.

Percy looked at the telescopic sight in disgust; he really couldn't see the point of it at all.

Chapter Thirty-Five

Cuthbert wandered vaguely into the village, and decided to drop in on Avril.

He knew she was in, because she sat with her back to the street behind a big window and he could see her.

His relationship with Avril was somewhat fraught. She always used those notebooks with a shiny spiral on top and Cuthbert was fascinated by them. He would stare at them and imagine a journey along the shiny wire from one end to the other.

The problem was that Avril tended to hold the book at the same height as her cleavage and this led to several misunderstandings in the past.

Cuthbert entered her office and she actually seemed pleased to see him. She smiled and insisted he sat with *them*. Cuthbert sat automatically and left his brain to sort out the puzzle of how two people had become *them*! His brain sent an itch to his shoulder and Cuthbert dutifully turned to scratch it and saw the man sitting in the corner.

Slumped, was a better description. The cares of the world had hammered this man into his chair and would never allow him to rise again. He gave a flick of his hand towards Cuthbert and resumed his critical examination of the carpet.

Avril seemed abnormally bright. She introduced Mr Pickles as a 'major contributor to the local paper' and assured Cuthbert his 'funny vegetable' photo's had the locals in stitches.

"Unfortunately," she added, "Mr Pickles was on his way over here with the best one yet, when he accidentally came up behind blind Pugh. The sheepdog could only see right behind himself and savaged the item destined for the front page."

Cuthbert gave Mr Pickles a sympathetic look and was rewarded with, "Never had much luck, from first thing in the morning to last thing at night, nothing but bad luck."

It was like being a psychiatrist to a depressed basset hound.

Cuthbert was moved to ask, "First thing in the morning?"

Mr Pickles nodded slowly. "From the minute I get up and fall over the wife's wooden leg. I warned her that there could be an accident and if she had to deal with Health and Safety, she wouldn't have a leg to stand on, but would she listen? No."

Cuthbert was startled by the crash of Avril's cup falling off the edge of the desk. She jumped up urgently spluttering, "Must go! That's the, er, signal that something important is about to happen somewhere else, at some time soon." She gathered her bag and journalistic excuses around her and made for the door.

"Bit like the 'Bat-signal' in Gotham City then?" asked Mr Pickles dourly.

"Yes, yes, it is," agreed Avril, closing the door behind her.

"Must cost a fortune in cups!" muttered Cuthbert suspiciously.

Mr Pickles droned on and on. Cuthbert had been brought up to be thoughtful and listened politely.

His father had always said, "Cuthbert, don't do to others anything you might regret doing to yourself. You may have to lay them out some day and you don't want them to take a bad opinion with them. We never know where they're going."

So, Cuthbert listened patiently, until he began to lose the will to live. He had been depressed himself from time to time, but as a farmer he would simply confide in his animals. He stopped that when one of his sheep tried to blow itself up using a stirrup pump.

Treading his weary way home after Avril returned and closed the office, Cuthbert realised he was seeing the world through different eyes.

Things were much clearer now. He had never noticed it before, but now that he looked close enough, that branch would be strong enough to hang his sorry self from.

Chapter Thirty-Six

Henry, Ronald and Percy sat at Cuthbert's table when he arrived home and had obviously been waiting for him.

The Captain arrived soon after and brought Elspeth and Margery with him.

Mugs of tea were passed down the table and the ladies tried to not look inside them too much.

Henry seemed concerned about Cuthbert and asked him, "Are you all right? It's getting us all down, you know, but if we stick together, we can solve this."

Cuthbert just nodded dejectedly.

The Captain asked, "You haven't spent time with Mr Pickles by any chance?"

Cuthbert nodded again.

A shudder ran around the table. Margery blushed slightly and said, "I had to ban him from the Mandrake Arms- he left everyone sitting staring into a glass contemplating suicide."

"That's rather harsh, Margery; was it difficult?" asked Elspeth.

Margery reddened again and admitted, "Well, I didn't actually *ban* him; I discouraged him."

Everyone stared and she was forced to explain. "I told him that the coat of arms on the sign outside meant that we were a branch of the Masons and he was only allowed in as a guest on the third week in August."

The men looked blank until Elspeth asked, "Isn't that when you go away on holiday, dear?"

Margery nodded.

"Don't blame you, old girl," barked the Captain. "Couldn't have had a man like that in the trenches, people would have been killed."

Margery opened her mouth, but caught a subtle shake of the head from Elspeth and didn't bother.

The scroll was rolled out and the women admired Percy's workmanship. Ronald had bashed the wax slug with his shoe until it looked more like the Great Seal of England after a very nasty experience.

Percy once again basked in the admiration, until he caught Cuthbert standing behind him with a tape measure. "What are you doing?" he asked in alarm.

Cuthbert measured his height and muttered, "Private commission," nodding towards Margery.

Margery smiled at Percy the way a hen-house owning fox would smile at his tenants.

It was agreed that substituting the scroll was the best plan so far. It was also the only plan and the only one they had bothered to write down. They needed an inside man to discover where the scroll was kept, as all the 'real' men still carried bruises from the last encounter and Margery's ample bosom wasn't easily disguised.

This had all been discussed privately. The Captain cleared his throat and addressed his wife. "Elspeth, dear," he began, "you know how sometimes we all have to make sacrifices and think of England, before we think of ourselves?"

"Of course I do, dear," answered Elspeth dreamily. Turning to Margery she said, "It was a lovely day, you know. My dress had been specially made and all the local children carried my train."

"Not that," snapped the Captain, before forcing himself to sound beguiling. "We need someone who can blend into the background and watch the brothers' Cool."

Elspeth looked at her husband aghast. "You mean like that time you asked me to infiltrate a harem to find out where the Maharaja kept his gold?"

The Captain coughed and spluttered, "That was for extra supplies, the horses were short of worm tablets."

"*Gold,*" whispered Percy indistinctly.

Elspeth continued, "Or the time you asked me to travel across the desert, the only white woman in an all male caravan, just to find out about the ancient City of Gold?"

"Gold," whispered Percy again.

The Captain was becoming exasperated; the wretched woman never said a word until you didn't want her to. "Yes, yes," he spluttered. "Will you do it?"

Elspeth milked the moment. "Whose gold are we after this time then?"

"Gold." whispered Percy for the third time.

"Is there something you would like to share with us, or are you going to make us wait an hour for the deathbed scene?" asked Margery silkily.

"I don't know what you mean," said Percy defensively.

"You said 'gold' three times," said Henry.

"No, I didn't," replied Percy, wriggling uncomfortably. "I said cold!" and he rubbed his arms briskly to make the point.

Ronald made an observation. "Percy, you are sitting with your back to the most diabolical heating device known to man." The cooking range hissed in acknowledgement. "Why would you say 'cold'?"

Percy looked around wildly. It was the kind of look which accelerates the thought process in other humans. The kind of look a hungry herd focuses on the weakest member at dinner time.

"Who were those two men in my cellar and where did those shovels come from?" asked Margery.

Percy's eyes flicked from side to side like ricocheting snooker balls.

Ronald then asked, "Why did we find a riddle in the cellar?"

Cuthbert giggled. "That was me. Someone told it to me and the white wall was the only place to write it down."

"Not that kind of *riddle,* you clot; a riddle for washing dirt out of rocks."

"Oh," said Cuthbert.

"That was you, Cuthbert?" purred Margery.

"Oh," said Cuthbert again.

Sometimes Percy loved to be the centre of attention, other times he would rather he wasn't. This was one of those times.

His interrogators persisted. "Wasn't one of them the postman?" asked the Captain. He turned to Henry. "You remember; that clot who was obsessed with some old goldmine?"

The oxygen was sucked out of the room as everyone took a deep breath. Things looked grim for a while, until they remembered to breathe out and put some back in.

"You've found gold!" accused Ronald.

"You weren't going to tell us, were you?" asked Henry.

"He will now!" snarled Margery.

"Which is the one with the stammer then?" Cuthbert asked.

Sweat began to bead on Percy's forehead as all eyes concentrated on him. He shuffled and racked his brains to come up with an interesting ancestor, but the pressure was too great and he gave up. With a resigned shrug, Percy explained the sequence of events that led to it all. Building the wooden fort had meant he needed a moat, so he diverted the stream, both depriving the mine of water and flooding Henry's cellar.

Margery hissed, "You *flooded* our cellar *and* wrecked it *getting rid of the water*?" Her hands clenched and the manicured nails started tapping across the table to get at him.

Percy gulped and thought that they could be a difficult audience, this Valley crowd. He explained how he found the mine, because he was trying to eat the crow and how he had lost the gold nugget when he was attacked by a forest.

A potted plant in the corner tittered and the Captain exclaimed, "Am*bush*ed, eh? Fiendishly clever tactic that."

The plant took a bow.

Ronald asked, "So the Valley mafia took the gold then?"

Percy nodded sadly.

Henry asked, "Was it real gold?"

Percy was about to shrug when Margery snapped, "Jasper!"

The plant in the corner replied, "The twins have that in hand. It's probably fool's gold, iron pyrites. The analysis has been held up because someone changed the locks on the school laboratory. They are probably in there even as we speak."

The Captain was puzzled. "Why fool's gold?"

Jasper answered, "Look who we took it from."

Heads nodded around the table and the Captain quickly muttered to the plant, "Do you do private analyses; I might have a problem."

The plant handed the Captain its card and all the attention returned to Percy.

"It's all for the best," said Percy desperately. "We can buy the Valley back."

"How many axes will that cost us?" asked Margery acidly.

Percy slumped.

Chapter Thirty-Seven

Madame Fifi gave the secret knock and waited for the door to click. Her hair had a new purple rinse and she patted it into place before she entered the room.

Concentrating on the swing of her hips, Madame Fifi sashayed across to where the Cool brothers sat beneath the tapestry. "Sorry to disturb you gentlemen," she breathed, "but there is a lady inquiring about a cleaning position."

The brothers looked at each other and one of them said, "We didn't advertise- she must have the wrong place. Please deal with it for us."

Madame Fifi lowered her voice. "I don't think she will take 'no' for an answer."

One of the brothers asked, "Is that her?"

Elspeth had entered behind the owner of the poodle parlour and was already dusting the wood panelling.

The brothers dismissed Madam Fifi without noticing her taste in head confection and one of them addressed Elspeth.

"This is a very private club, madam. We did not advertise for a cleaner. Would you please leave?"

Elspeth dusted her way along the wall and showed them the dreadful black smear on the cloth. "You won't be private for long, gentlemen, after the first Cholera epidemic."

The two men sat upright. "Cholera!" they barked in unison.

"Oh, yes," replied Elspeth. "I've seen it all before, sirs. It starts with a little neglect and before you know it, bodies all over the place. Building cordoned off, police everywhere dressed in white paper suits and spacemen disinfecting *everything*."

"Police!" said one brother.

"*Everything?*" spluttered the other brother.

Not so cool now, are we, thought Elspeth as they conferred.

After much muttering and nodding, one of the Cool brothers said, "All right then. Twice a week at standard rates." He leaned forward for emphasis as he insisted, "On no account must you touch the tapestry, understood?"

Elspeth nodded as she stared at the huge representation of dragons battling to conquer heaven, and replied, "Oh yes, understood, dear. Dry clean only, is it?"

Ronald set up his laptop and tapped in his security codes. He carried spare batteries for everything due to the Valley's allergic reaction to electricity. He coupled the speakers up and left everything 'hands free'.

Henry, Percy, the Captain and Cuthbert watched in fascination. The lap-top showed a map and a green dot winked at them periodically.

The speakers crackled slightly. "Sound-test, level reading?"

Ronald sat up straight and whispered, "Stand by. Level four."

The crackle decreased as Elspeth adjusted something and the next message was clear. "Both x-rays have left the building. Both are foxtrot! We have a cordon-sanitaire, stand by."

The Captain barked, "The woman's gone mad, it's all too much for her. Call her back in!"

Ronald shushed him to say, "She's spot on; she's just told me that the Cool brothers have gone out and they are walking, and the Valley mafia have the perimeter. No-one can approach the door without being seen."

The next voice was Jasper's, demonstrating his skills at surveillance codes and techniques. "Red Vauxhall, Tango-Lima- Echo-One-Four-Five-Whiskey; two up, both x-rays going south from blue one through to blue four."

Ronald whispered, "Roger that."

Elspeth whispered, "Roger that also."

Henry looked impressed. "Isn't it amazing what the little chaps pick up at school?"

Percy was hanging on to every word and Cuthbert was listening to music inside his head.

Elspeth carefully inspected the tapestry. She felt around the back for contact pads or wires and when she was happy, lifted one corner and peered behind it.

There in the middle of the wall was an old fashioned safe with a combination dial.

Elspeth smiled and removed a hair grip from her bun and set to work.

Ronald sat tensed as the sound of Elspeth's commentary filled Cuthbert's kitchen.

"It's a Grainger, model six. Good job it's not the eight or we would need some jelly."

"They having a party?" asked Percy suspiciously.

Ronald muttered absently, "Gelignite, nit-wit."

Percy filed this away for some adventure in the future.

Elspeth was calm and collected, even when the door crashed open and a voice cried, "I knew you were too good to be true, what are you doing and who said you could bring a pot plant in here *Aaaaaargghh!*"

Elspeth calmly mentioned that a "threat had been neutralised" and Jasper came on air asking for "two men and a body bag."

"Good grief, Captain!" yelled Ronald in delight. "What did your wife do before you met her?"

The Captain looked puzzled and said slowly, "She said she was an Agent Provocateur; I thought it meant she modelled underwear."

Margery had appeared through one of Cuthbert's secret panels just before the team returned from the operation.

She listened to a recording of the night's work and raised an eyebrow as Elspeth 'sanitised the scene, re-locked all doors and dismantled the cordon in stages to allow maximum surveillance during withdrawal.'

"That didn't come from the women's institute booklet," she said.

The team entered shortly after. Actually, Elspeth, Jasper, two bushes and a large sack entered. The sack was dumped upright in a chair and the two bushes left.

Jasper and Elspeth gratefully accepted steaming mugs of tea and gave an after-ops report to Ronald.

The sack wriggled and emitted muffled squeaks when Percy poked it.

"Right," said Ronald, "whose the old bag?"

Jasper slit the top and allowed the material to fall.

Beneath a purple explosion were two blazing eyes and a mouth gagged with one of the dog collars from her parlour.

"Madam Fifi?" exclaimed Henry.

"Madam Fifi, my foot," snorted Margery. "She was Rosie Cleghorn at school, and she had no colour sense then either."

Ronald inspected the captive carefully. "Will she be a problem?"

Margery thought for a moment and then laughed. "The mafia have copies of all the fake Kennel Club documents she has produced over the years. The last 'Best of Breed' was in fact the result of a midnight encounter between 'Persephone of Alexandria' and Blind-Pugh. The silly bitch was lucky she approached him from the right angle."

She watched Fifi's shoulders slump and the blaze in her eyes diminish before adding, "Let her collect her clippers and move on, before Constable Beeching gets stuck in her doorway."

After the prisoner had gone, Ronald turned to Elspeth. "Nice work that; if ever the dusting gets too much, give me a call."

Elspeth inclined her head gracefully and turned to Henry as he asked, "Well, did you get it?"

She slid a sheet of paper out from her sleeve. "This is a receipt for the deeds; they have sent them to Bogus, Sharp and Shifty for safe keeping, if you'll pardon the pun." She then laid Percy's fake deed roll on the table. "I can always apply for a job there, I suppose."

Margery patted Elspeth's shoulder in a comradely gesture. "There might be another way, dear. Geraldine is on intimate terms with either one or all of the partners- she's not sure at the moment."

Henry gaped and asked, "Is anyone in this Valley the person I thought they were?"

Margery smiled secretively. "We don't know, dear. Are *you* the person *you thought you were?*"

Chapter Thirty-Eight

Percy approached the mine entrance and paused as he wondered if he should knock, but a hole in a rock-face didn't provide many opportunities, so he just entered.

Choosing a candle stub, he lit it and held it aloft. Stepping over the railway sleepers, he made his way deeper into the workings, and the rhythmic chink of pick points on rock became louder.

Turning the last corner into the working gallery, he was astounded to see the crow sat there on a specially made perch.

"Polly!" he said, and promptly plunged himself into utter blackness. Some words cannot safely be uttered near a candle flame!

After being savaged in the dark, Percy realised there were also words which cannot be safely uttered near a crow.

Scrabbling about, he accepted a light from one of the miners who came back to see who had upset the canary.

"What canary?" asked Percy, massaging the peck marks on his nose and glowering at the crow.

The miner looked sheepish as he explained that "all mines had small birds in the workings to detect gas." With a shrug, he acknowledged that the crow was all they had got, but "anyway," he insisted, "he is company."

Percy explained that "persons or people unknown had let slip the news about the gold mine and that the sample was being analysed."

"What sample?" asked one miner.

"What people person?" the other one queried.

Percy rolled his eyes theatrically and insisted "this is not the time to apportion blame; it is time to move on and put the past behind us."

"It was you, wasn't it?" asked the other miner.

The first miner shrieked, "What sample?"

Percy explained that the nugget had fallen from the rock face and accidentally somersaulted into his welly. Unfortunately, he had been bushwhacked on the way home and the rock was stolen.

"How did you know?" demanded the first miner.

"Know what?" asked Percy.

"If it was in there by accident, how did you know it had gone when you didn't know it had been?"

Percy gaped. He would have to watch this one.

As they walked back towards the outside world and sunshine, Percy was very conscious of two things. One, the crow rode on the shoulder of the first miner instead of his, and two; both miners were still carrying their picks.

He said, "There's no need to panic. We don't know whether the mafia can actually assay the sample and we don't know if they could recognise the result if it fell on them."

They entered sunlight to cries of "Halt, stand still! Drop your weapons!" and "Check the scruffy one's wellies!"

Lying flat on his face with a Valley mafia enforcer on his back, the first miner gasped, "I think we can assume that the results are in."

The roaring of chainsaws was only interrupted by a 'zing' as another tree was severed from its roots and began to fall.

The Cool brothers watched as the work teams started clearing the ground opposite Percy's fort.

The brothers agreed that the little twerp hadn't done too badly working on his own, especially with the handicap of being who he was. They also noted enviously that there was no water this side of the Valley, so they would not have a moat.

Still, the whole idea of the battle would be to take Percy's fort and then they could refuse to give it back.

This made them both chuckle.

Finding himself sitting between the two miners, Percy made an attempt at humour. "A rose between thorns, eh lads?" he quipped.

No-one replied.

Chapter Thirty-Nine

Along the other side of Cuthbert's table were most of the grim faced inhabitants of the Valley.

Jasper observed, "The condemned man has a sense of humour methinks."

Margery nudged him and chided, "He's innocent until I have found him guilty, remember, Jasper?"

Henry coughed discreetly. "I meant to ask, my dear; exactly when did we vote on who was to be the judge?"

Margery smiled at her husband and waved a hand dismissively. "Oh, I don't bother you with all the tiresome details of everyday life, dear."

Henry took the hint, but the Captain barked, "Damned strange, if you ask me! We men make all the decisions of importance and yet suddenly a woman takes charge of this?"

Margery's voice slipped between her lips with all the fascination and danger of a snake's tongue. "What decisions were *those* ones, Captain?" she asked smoothly.

The Captain looked around for support, but all the other men suddenly seemed fascinated by the architecture of Cuthbert's ceiling.

"Well," he tried, "twenty-four hour drinking at the Mandrake Arms for a start."

"And?" prompted Margery.

The Captain began counting on his fingers. "Extra beer deliveries, a pavement drinking area for summer, and 'two for the price of one' between 6 p.m. and 10 p.m. at weekends."

"And how many of those suggestions have actually borne fruit, Captain?" purred Margery.

"Well, actually, er, none really," he conceded, before snapping at his friend Henry, "I thought you made all the major decisions in your house?"

Henry rubbed his chin thoughtfully and replied, "Oh, I do, I really do, but I never know which ones I have permission to implement."

Percy saw an opening. "Right, well, we don't want to be involved in a domestic, now do we, lads; we'll be on our way." He stood and made to leave, but the chair seemed determined to leave with him.

The mafia had put a front chair leg into each of his wellies when they had sat him down.

Percy sighed and decided to pay attention.

Margery held quite an unconventional court. It mostly consisted of asking everyone for their worst 'Percy stories' and proving that he was actually to blame for everything anyone could think of.

Percy tried to object several times, but was ignored. Finally, he lost his temper and shouted, "I am trying to be objectionable, your honour-ship!"

Margery deigned to glance his way and assured him he had succeeded beyond his wildest dreams, so he sat again, quite pleased with himself.

Percy asked Margery to repeat the verdict. The first time it sounded like "Shear a fawn." The second time it came across as "Sound a horn." The third repeat was even more ridiculous, "Shot at Dawn!"

Everyone gasped, but Margery was adamant that everyone was entitled to their five minutes of fame and Percy would go out with a bang.

As the mafia marched him out between them, Percy had one tactic left. His shoulders slumped and he muttered, "Manage without the gold then."

The room went silent.

Margery asked, "What did you say?"

Percy looked around in puzzlement. "Sorry, I was just wondering who else had found some gold."

Margery glared at the two miners, who simply shrugged. She stood with her knuckles whitening as she gripped the edge of the table. "Are you telling me that the only person to find any gold in a gold mine is this miserable little reprobate and if we want some we have to ask *him*?"

Percy looked directly at her and said, "Dunno about him, but you could always ask *me*."

The miners whispered to Percy so that the mafia guards wouldn't hear, "Right then, where did you find it?"

112

Percy pointed to the wall just above where he had found the piece of rock. The two miners attacked the rock face until they stood panting for breath.

"Are you sure?" gasped one of them.

Percy scratched his helmet and admitted, "It might have been over there."

The miners attacked the new spot with renewed frenzy until they had to lean on each other for support.

"What did it look like?" asked the other miner between short ragged breaths.

Percy held two fingers apart and said, "Oh, about this big with a tiny glittery bit off to one side."

"What?" snapped the first miner, exploring Percy's neck with his fingers; they felt an empty clasp on a cheap chain. "You fool, that was the standard nugget we would have judged our finds with. Every gold miner carries one!"

"I don't," said the other miner.

"Well, neither do I now!" screamed his colleague.

Chapter Forty

Geraldine entered the offices of Bogus, Sharp and Shifty. She wasn't over thrilled by the assignment, but everyone else had played a part in not achieving anything, so it must be her turn.

The receptionist gave her a quick appraisal to anticipate either revenue or trouble, and smiled sweetly, having assumed that it would be a divorce.

When they didn't smile as they entered, it usually was a divorce and, if they were beaming when they left, they had been told how much they would make out of it.

Geraldine tapped on the glass pane of the solicitor's door; gilt letters announced that Mr Bogus may lurk here.

She opened the door and tried to spot someone amongst the piles of paper. It was stacked up on the desk, on the floor, and on the window sills.

A huge newspaper flapped and rustled amongst it all and a face appeared briefly. A voice said, "Take a seat, give me the villain's name and the brief shall set you free."

Geraldine remained standing. A face gradually came into view as the newspaper was lowered slowly.

The man studied Geraldine with a worried frown. "Are you from the Bookies?" he asked and the newspaper trembled slightly.

Geraldine assured him that she wasn't and asked if he remembered their University leaving do.

The man's eyes widened. "You're not, are you?"

Geraldine snapped impatiently, "If I was, it would be sixteen now, you fool."

"Yes, I suppose it would." He put down his paper sheepishly and Geraldine noticed it was 'The Racing Times'. He studied her again and admitted, "I don't really remember much about it. Were you the one who came dressed as a penguin?"

Geraldine sighed. "That was the Mother Superior from the convent next door; she wanted some of her nuns back."

The newspaper was beginning to rise again, so Geraldine tried, "Ever heard of Sledgehammer?"

The man snorted, "Not into D.I.Y. at all, I'm afraid."

Geraldine left and entered the next office down the hall and ducked as a feathered missile hummed past her ear to embed itself in the corridor wall behind her.

This man seemed to have had his ears surgically enhanced to hold extra darts.

He peered myopically at his visitor and asked, "Have you moved the board?"

Geraldine entered cautiously and asked "Do the words Sledgehammer, Cool or Cuthbert mean anything to you?"

He frowned. "Is that the firm who took our secretary from us? If I ever come face to face with any of them, I'll, I'll ..."

"Yes?" asked Geraldine.

"I'll wave a writ at them!" he spluttered.

Geraldine retreated as the man reached for a fresh dart.

The last door bore the legend 'Mr Shifty'.

Geraldine knocked, received a reply and entered.

A tall handsome man stood and came around the desk to shake her hand and bade her to take a chair.

This is more like it, thought Geraldine. She outlined her request and their possible history and the man listened intently.

Eventually he said, "Scroll, eh? We don't see many of those these days. It would definitely have come through me; the others just have rich fathers, so we keep them amused. I actually don't remember the 'leaving do' as I was a bit of a swot. In fact it was me who phoned the Mother Superior, so I was probably on 'Fire Patrol' instead."

He promised to make some enquiries and Geraldine left.

Mr Shifty stroked his chin and stood at his window watching her cross the street.

Picking up his phone he said, "Mr Cool, please."

The Cool brothers glanced at each other as one of them replaced the phone. They both nodded and stood.

"Cleaning lady," said one of them, "we are going out for a while. Lock up after yourself, please."

"Right you are, dear," said Elspeth.

After the door closed, Elspeth busied herself over the big scale model of the proposed theme park.

Slicing away part of a papier-mâché hilltop, she inserted a microphone. "Testing, reading please."

"Strength four," replied Ronald in her ear piece.

The next one went into a fold around the seam of the tapestry and the third went under the desk where it would be spotted easily.

When the brothers returned, she emerged from under the desk holding a small plastic grille by its wire. "I don't know what this is, sirs. I thought it was a mouse!" She handed it over.

The brothers' eyes widened. "More like a mole, cleaning lady. I think we have discovered the leak," one of them said to the other.

"You just point me at it, sir," said Elspeth. "Have it cleaned up in no time."

The brothers patiently explained that information had left the office and this was the explanation.

Elspeth frowned in concentration as she asked, "I wonder if that nice Mrs Fifi saw anyone come in?"

The brothers nodded in agreement and added, "We haven't seen her lately; perhaps you had better have your own key, cleaning lady."

Ronald discreetly watched Elspeth. She was helping him with an inventory of weapons and equipment ready for the forthcoming showdown.

They had formed quite a close bond over the radio. All surveillance people were prone to this; they began to trust each other and bond.

Obviously, Elspeth was a bit out-of-date with some of the modern weapons, but Ronald would bring her up to speed.

Even he was taken by surprise when she asked, "Have we got any claymores?"

Ronald nodded over to a box in the corner full of anti-personnel mines. He was impressed.

Elspeth rummaged and threw one to the side. "Not these! I meant those big Scottish swords that can take a man's head off." She wandered back to her desk.

Ronald brought his heartbeat back under control as he watched the anti-personnel mine bounce into a corner. After the thought of several hundred explosive propelled ball bearings spring cleaning the room for them retreated, he relaxed.

Nobody ever found a role for Cuthbert around anything dangerous and he had always been quite offended by this. After all, he had never knowingly killed anyone. If they weren't ready to be buried when he got them, it was hardly his fault, was it?

He sauntered into the outbuilding to offer Ronald and Elspeth a cup of tea and picked up the discarded mine. Stroking its shiny curved surface, he read, 'Face towards the enemy'.

"Oh, is it a camera?" he asked, before pulling the string.

Elspeth's hearing was partly protected by the ear-piece she still wore, but Ronald thought his ear-drums had been fitted with cymbals. The ringing rattling sound was everywhere.

The carefully invoiced stack of equipment had been reduced to mulch and was distributed across the farmyard along with the wall it had been stacked against.

Cuthbert still held the claymore canister in his hands ready to wind the film on ready for the next photo and decided to take it with him, removing two pieces of evidence at once.

Percy had wandered deeper into the workings to let everyone calm down.

One of the miners wanted to leave him in the dark, saying, "He isn't worth a candle."

The other one said, "He wouldn't make a good one, if we melted him down."

Percy smiled and shook his head. The camaraderie of miners!

Some of the workings looked really old and he was looking for the tunnel that went under his fort. His wellies slapped reassuringly in the gloom as he walked. The little railway line had ended some time ago and Percy saw a gleam up ahead.

He hurried forward and saw the hole he and the blackbird had fallen into. He had found his fort. He had also found the source of the gleam; the light was shining onto a sparkling seam of gold. The water Percy had allowed to flood down to the Mandrake Arms had washed part of the tunnel wall away and revealed it.

Percy stared at it and then he stroked it. It was hard to resist licking it. He jabbered to himself like a mad man. "Fool's gold, eh! Percy's gold, more like!"

He soon discovered that his own name was one of those words disliked by candles, as he stood in the dark again.

Jasper and Margery entered the outbuilding looking for Henry just as Ronald and Elspeth's hearing returned. Margery looked at the missing wall and merely raised an eyebrow.

Jasper had to comment. "French doors and a patio, is it?" he asked with a smirk.

"Don't any of these Valley kids go to school?" growled Ronald.

Margery ruffled Jasper's hair and replied, "My twins went to school- do you remember the twins?" she asked sweetly as a shudder went around the room.

Everyone remembered the twins.

"I remember one day," she continued wistfully, "I had a new boyfriend and I rang the school to ask where the twins had hidden him. As the receptionist was dealing with me, she suddenly screamed, 'North gate, pupil escaping!' Then the alarm sounded and a team was sent out. When the receptionist came back on she said, 'It's OK, the dogs got him. Now, where were we?"

Margery shook her head at the recollection.

"Was it one of the twins?" asked Elspeth, full of concern.

Margery smiled and said, "Good Lord, no, apparently it was 'Sucker' Simpson. The twins had convinced him that any dog bites would criss-cross eventually and the scars would look like tattoos. So every time he distracted the dogs, the twins would use the tunnel instead."

Ronald shook his head, and discovered a post-explosion headache.

Jasper looked on admiringly and Elspeth rolled up her sleeves. "Right," she said, "I'll need a large mixing bowl and several wooden spoons."

Ronald growled again. "This is no time to bake a blooming cake."

Elspeth gave him a dangerous look before she replied, "Your supply of explosives seems to have distributed itself across several acres. Mine is still in the cupboard under the sink."

Jasper nudged Ronald. "What happened anyway?" he asked.

Ronald blew out his cheeks, sat back and replied, "Well, we're in Cuthbert's outbuilding on Cuthbert's farm; does that narrow it down a bit?"

"Percy?" suggested Jasper.

"Probably!" said Ronald.

Percy sat on the tunnel floor. He had filled one welly with grains of gold and he poured them out in a stream, giggling.

At last, his various personalities were coming in handy; he could argue the pros and cons without giving away the secret.

"I could buy back the Valley!" decided one voice.

"Why should I?" argued the second voice.

"You would be everyone's landlord!" suggested a third.

Percy was fascinated; it was like being part of a quorum, except he didn't know who the others were.

Marvin hung onto the dashboard grimly.

The van lurched first one way and then the other. The shock of banging against the sides was bad enough, but every time the van hit a bump, he caught a whiff of the road gang in the back. They were heading up the Valley to where all the illegal excavations and diggings were rumoured to be happening.

Motor vehicles didn't seem to be regular visitors along here and the van desperately tried to fit into the track marks of some sort of digger. In the back, One-Lung Louie flew sideways for the umpteenth time and bounced off Swivelling Simon coming the other way.

Buster simply stood braced in the middle and let his broad shoulders rock slightly every time the drains inspector shouted "Sorry, lads!" as he hit the ruts edge on once again.

Marvin concentrated on not smashing his teeth together as he ordered, "Pull up at that chap with the red and white pole; he looks official."

The van gave a last lurch sideways as the drains inspector stopped and they all tumbled out in undisguised relief.

Marvin adopted an official stance and addressed the youth with the pole. The lad's eyes were closed and his hair swung to some tinny rhythm coming from his ear. One knee seemed to twitch in one direction, just before the other one took over in the opposite one. Marvin was just about to reach out and tap the lad on his shoulder, when the youth let out a yell and swung his pole wildly, nearly decapitating Marvin in the process.

Winston swung his 'air guitar' as his favourite cacophony reached its crescendo. He opened his eyes to acknowledge the audience and blinked in amazement when he found he *actually had one*.

A man who looked incredibly like a council official gaped at him with one hand raised for self-defence purposes.

Behind him was an assortment from Madame Tussaud's.

One of them wheezed like an old set of bagpipes; another one watched his muscles ripple and the third one's eye swivelled alarmingly.

"Whoa, dude," said Winston, "you nearly bent my pole."

Marvin lowered his arm and stepped forward. "I am a council official and demand to see the man in charge."

"Cool," replied Winston, still nodding to the music. "Yes, that's him."

"Is he here?" snapped Marvin, wishing his wife *Doreeen* could see him being masterful.

"Is who here?" asked Winston, still jigging.

Marvin repeated the name, "Cool, Mister Cool!"

Winston mentally overlaid the music with the conversation and replied, "It sure is cool, mister, real cool."

Marvin felt his jaw sag and looked at his team for assistance.

One-Lung Louie glanced around for someone sensible and spotted the sunlight flash on the surveyor's lens. "Sniper!" he screamed. "Get down!"

Using his own bodyweight, Louie rugby tackled Marvin in a heroic act of self-sacrifice.

Marvin went down like a sack of potatoes grabbed by the ankles and landed flat in a patch of mud. *Someone really must ask Louie how he lost that lung,* he thought, straining a gritty mixture from between his teeth.

The surveyor ambled over to ask Winston why he had surveyed the same spot seven times in the last hour, and paused as all eyes turned to him.

Chapter Forty-One

Margery watched Elspeth carefully as her friend weighed out various innocuous ingredients into a huge bowl. Margery considered her opening question and decided upon, "Not the ordinary set of talents a housewife would expect to pick up, is it, Elspeth dear?"

Elspeth concentrated as she poured some of Cuthbert's fertiliser into the bowl, then she answered, "But I was an *army wife,* Margery; we were expected to nod politely as the commanding officer's wife waffled on and baked endless cakes for charity."

"Not like that one, I hope," said Margery, nodding towards the bowl.

Elspeth smiled. "We picked up a lot of the jargon and the military's passion for acronyms can be fascinating; it makes for quite a parlour game. For instance, the Special Air Service wives were known as 'Sane And Sensible' compared to their husbands who ran around in gas masks assaulting empty buildings all day. Imagine cooking dinner for a man exhausted from exactly the same games as his children played all day?"

Margery waited patiently as Elspeth's memories went along their torturous paths. "When we were posted abroad, we women often pretended to go shopping, and studied the locals. We never let on that we spoke the lingo, you know, and achieved a lot more than our husbands *ever* did at a road block annoying people all day."

Margery was impressed. "Did you receive any recognition?"

"Not really, dear. Between the Official Secrets Act, the Geneva Convention and the need to appear as 'the little woman', we treated it as a diversion. But I will tell you this."

Margery leaned in closer.

"Waterloo would have been very different with rock-cakes and a mixture very similar to this!"

Marvin borrowed the surveyor's telescopic ladder and scaled the wall of Percy's wooden fort. He walked around the ramparts whilst his team also climbed over and joined him.

They dropped to the inner floor and Marvin announced, "This is definitely an illegal construction, gentlemen."

Louie looked around to see who else had climbed over!

"And if that is a hole, then we have an illegal excavation as well," Marvin added.

Percy heard voices that weren't the ones he had been arguing with in his head. He poured the gold dust into a pile and scooped soil and grass over it; then he popped his head out. "What are you doing in my fort?" he shouted.

The invaders jumped guiltily and Marvin announced pompously, "You, sir, are in violation of several restrictive regulations, and I haven't even considered those wellies yet."

Percy raised himself to his full height, which wasn't very impressive, as he stood in a hole, and said, "Consider yourselves in the presence of a future Dragon Dropping, gentlemen, and *beware*."

He gave the twisting wrist sign as he opened the invisible safe and to his amazement, two people returned the gesture.

All of Winston's audio receptors were fully engaged, but his fringe had blown to one side, just in time to react to Percy's sign. He was no real surprise, but One-Lung Louie certainly was.

Louie spluttered as everyone focused on him. "Well, I haven't got the breath for many sports now, have I?" he asked plaintively. "Three days rolling dice and moving little plastic men fits the bill just right."

Percy clambered out of his hole and stepped towards his new comrades, Winston was involved in a particularly difficult invisible guitar riff and couldn't be disturbed, but Louie accepted the secret handshake with a puzzled look … because Percy had just made it up.

A voice from the parapet made everyone turn and look upward. "You people are trespassing and you must leave, now!"

The Cool brothers gazed down from their commanding height.

Marvin stared up at them. "The Local Authority *cannot* trespass; we give permission for all purchases, alterations and maintenance of land. You, sir, merely own property under our supervision for future generations."

Percy chirped in, "Now you've done it- that's a Great Dragon Dropping, that is."

"They're not going to do it from up there, are they?" asked Swivelling Simon, trying to keep an eye on both of them at once.

One Cool brother turned to the other and commanded, "Send in the dogs!"

Percy, Marvin, Winston and the road gang were suddenly very aware they were all inside a circular enclosure with nowhere to go. The sound of barking outside lent an urgency to the situation, and Percy cried, "Down the hole, quickly! We'll escape through the mine."

Each one of them entered the hole quickly, but in very different ways. The adventurous went head first, the leaders allowed lesser mortals to go ahead to trigger traps and Winston dangled for a while until he let go of the pole.

The escapees scampered down the tunnel as if the hounds of hell were after them and on the parapet the Cool brothers patted two poodles from Aunt Fifi's abandoned parlour.

Percy led the way into what was obviously the cellar of the Mandrake Arms. People fell gasping across barrels and boxes, and the fittest barricaded the opening.

"This isn't a mine," gasped Simon, looking strangely at Percy.

"Nobody said it was," wheezed Percy.

"Yes, you did," contributed Marvin. "You said 'down the hole, we'll go through the *mine*'."

Percy thought quickly. "No, what I said was, 'we need a hole, *use mine*'."

Everyone watched Percy closely; why was he being so evasive, why was he covering something up and most of all, why did he have glitter all over his clothing?

The Cool brothers stood side by side and stared over the Valley. They agreed that it was a beautiful spot and they admired the trees and the silence. Then one of them gave the signal and the excavators and chain saws began their symphony.

Marvin had written several furious e-mails to the Mayor's office and to the High Sheriff and even to the Prime Minister. Then he wrote one to every main newspaper in the land.

His secretary intercepted them on her computer as usual and simply sent one yellow post-it note to the planning board as she always did.

The Valley rang to the sound of excavators and shouted instructions.

The Cool brothers cast envious eyes over Percy's fort and were actually copying it.

Each fort had a digger beside it to raise mounds and dig ditches and defence works; the arms swung and lifted like a scorpion's tail. This would be the ultimate Sledgehammer battle site, they would attract thousands of fans, all dressed in character, and they would be forced to buy food, drink and merchandise as they entered.

The Cool brothers couldn't have been happier if they sat on a gold mine!

Chapter Forty-Two

Percy was in a corner of the bar of the Mandrake Arms. He sat alone, just a bench, a table and a Percy.

He closed his eyes and imagined a hammock between two palm trees and his wellies proudly on the hot sands.

The bench sagged slightly to his left as someone joined him. Then it sagged to the right as someone else sat.

Percy sighed. *So much for a quiet moment*, he thought.

Opening his eyes, Percy was surprised to find Jasper opposite him and a member of the Valley mafia on each side of him.

Jasper stared and Percy automatically went through a mental catalogue of all the things he was hiding. Life was simply too short, so he gave up.

Percy needed to control the situation, whatever it was, so he said, "Here, aren't you lot too young to come in here?"

Jasper smiled and replied, "If wisdom really came with age, you would have more sense than to mention that."

Percy furrowed his brow and wisely kept quiet.

"Dandruff, is it?" asked Jasper.

Percy held his breath as one of the mafia brushed his hand over his shoulder and displayed the result before tipping the grains onto the table. They glittered. Percy glanced around the room and felt the bodies each side of him increase the pressure. *I'm being leaned on,* he thought.

Jasper watched Percy carefully; sweat caused streaks in the glitter on his forehead and his eyes slid from side to side. This was a man dreaming of a future in the sun. This was a man with independent means. *This* was a potential contributor to mafia funds.

Jasper smiled.

Margery was shocked to discover she was visiting every room in the Mandrake Arms as if she were saying goodbye to it. She had found real happiness here with Henry and even some of the Valley folk were beginning to seem normal.

She caught sight of Jasper and two of his little friends tormenting Percy, but as they weren't drinking, it seemed harmless enough. She wandered down to the cellar and stopped in utter amazement. Her cellar was full of people and some of them were drawing on her white walls.

Marvin quickly came over and steered Margery away by the arm and explained things to her. It seemed, at the rate the Cool brothers were progressing, they would complete the theme park before the Council organised enough scones for a planning meeting. Then they would be in 'retrospective planning territory'. Marvin shuddered at the thought. This is why the Local Authority demanded notice of building works, so that they had months in which to find ways to say no.

Applying for retrospective planning permission was fraught with difficulty for the Authority. By the time something was built, even the public could see that it was probably a good idea and ask, "What's the point of knocking it down?" This was precisely why the public wasn't given an opinion in the first place.

Margery looked at the impromptu plans drawn on her walls, with the forts in black and the proposed attack routes marked in red and splashes of green for the trees. It began to look like a 'Jackson Pollock'.

Percy came down looking furtively over his shoulder, but the mafia stayed upstairs. They weren't worried, they knew where he lived. Percy studied the drawing and listened to the plans for holding up the work or cancelling it altogether.

"Too late!" he announced in a superior fashion. "There's no stopping us now."

"What do you mean *us*?" asked Swivelling Simon.

Percy smirked. "By the time YOU lot get organised, the park will be ready and I will be a Great Dragon Dropping."

"As opposed to a camel dropping, I presume?" Sneered Ronald from the cellar steps behind Percy. "Do you really think they need you now?" he pressed. "You've already given them the Valley and built one of the forts; what do they want you for- helmet-maker to the stars?"

Percy fumed, but Ronald would not give up. "Come back to Cuthbert's, the lot of you. We should hear something interesting tonight."

They all began to follow him up the stairs. Percy brought up the rear grumbling all the way.

The atmosphere in Cuthbert's kitchen was tense. With the heat from the cooking range combined with the stench from the road gangs' overalls it was soon a 'men only' gathering.

Everyone gathered around Ronald's surveillance equipment as it hummed into life and various coloured lights danced about until they settled into a pattern. The speakers hissed and then cleared.

"Oh, this is a wonderful model, you gentlemen *are* clever." Elspeth's tortured cleaning lady's vowels came through loud and clear as she pretend-dusted the model of the Valley. "Are all the houses exactly like the real Valley?" she asked.

One of the Cool brothers replied, "Oh, yes, our surveyor was thorough. You see that jumble of huts, sheds, thatch and pig-stys? That mess belongs to a chap called Cuthbert."

The men assembled in the room glanced upwards nervously as if they would see two giant eyeballs in the sky watching them.

The other Cool brother said, "Not now it doesn't, brother; that mess belongs to us." They both giggled.

Elspeth's voice came again. "Oh, look, there's even a little sign hanging outside the pub."

A scratching sound came from the speakers as a Cool brother rubbed his hands together and said, "That will be a real money spinner for us; we will turn it into a theme pub with 'Ogre night' and Troll cocktails."

"Over my dead body," muttered Marjorie; holding her nose behind the wood panelling.

Percy looked around smugly. "Told you it was too late. Even the Post Office will issue its own stamps with Sledgehammer characters on them."

Ronald shushed him and said, "Wait, my agent knows what she is doing."

The Captain bridled. His agent? The Captain thought she was *his* agent? *Have to watch this fellow,* he thought.

Elspeth could be heard again. "So everyone in the Valley will be working for you then, gentlemen?"

A louder rubbing, crackling sound was heard as the Cool brothers laughed. "Some of them might be acceptable in costume- that Margery would look nice selling oranges."

"Over my *nice*, dead body," muttered Margery again.

The voices continued. "Most of them seem simply unreliable. We haven't figured out what any of them actually *do*."

Most of the men nodded happily at this.

"It must have been difficult getting planning permission for all this, though?" asked Elspeth silkily.

It sounded as if the laughter would cause serious breathing problems this time.

"Oh, my dear," came a voice, "planning permission is for people who don't really own anything. We own everything. After free tickets for his son and an 'Honorary Warlock' post, we even own the Mayor!"

Marvin recoiled in horror. "My messages!" he cried. "I tried to alert the Mayor; I'm doomed."

The drains inspector patted him on the shoulder and confided, "Don't worry, boss; your secretary never sends your messages and the 'post-it' note blew off a desk in planning and went into the bin."

Marvin was flooded with relief and gratitude; then he was flooded with anger and resentment; then relief battled successfully with anger whilst gratitude choked resentment and he achieved a weird sort of equilibrium.

Percy crowed, "Told you we've got it all covered."

Elspeth made all the right noises before she asked, "I suppose some local help made it all possible though?"

Everyone tensed at the sudden silence- had Elspeth gone too far?

A voice barked, "I hope you don't mean that scruffy little chap who thinks he will be the next Dragon Dropping? What would *we* do with someone stupid enough to give away someone else's Valley?"

Percy gaped at the lap-top as if it was flapping its lid and speaking to him personally. His hands clenched and his helmet felt very tight.

The other brother spoke. "We thought about using him for the body on the gallows, but crows seem to sit on his shoulder, even *they* won't peck at him. No, as soon as we take his fort in the first battle, he will be sent into exile."

Percy frantically pulled his copy of 'Sledgehammer for less-than-nerds' out of his welly and skimmed through the pages. "Exile? That's not even a town in the Sledgehammer kingdom!" he wailed.

Chapter Forty-Three

Cuthbert wandered around his farmyard, looking at all the jobs he had meant to do over the years. He was also keeping an eye out for the Cool brothers watching him from above!

He rattled the gate on the bull-pen; he never repaired it after the bull escaped all that time ago, just in case someone gave him another and he needed to get rid of that one too.

The hen-house was silent and had been since he fixed the door several months ago. They were certainly safe, he thought. They had been inside when he nailed it shut.

Cuthbert viewed his embalming room with all its tubes, pipes and bodies. "Good grief!" he exclaimed. "How long have they been there?"

His shoulders slumped; it was all someone else's problem now.

Percy tugged at his helmet, but it wouldn't budge. His red hair had sprouted inside it, until it almost floated above him. He attacked the huge thistles outside his shed; if he was going to have to move, no-one else would have his prize blooms.

Elspeth dusted her shelves and sighed. She had enjoyed all the subterfuge and it was good to have a role in life again.

None of her edge was had lost and she could still show the men a thing or two. Yes, it was good to be a vital part of something, where decisions meant life or death and the adrenaline flowed. But, my, how the dust built up behind you.

The Cool brothers were adding scale forts to the opposing sides of the Valley to keep the model up to date. "Do you think this Cuthbert will be any trouble?" one of them asked.

The other one looked up. "No, not at all." he replied. "He's a kind of accidental tourist; he wanders through life without causing a ripple. No-one notices him; if he bumps into you, all you remember is that some chap said 'excuse me'."

Cuthbert stared at Ronald's infernal eaves-dropping machine on his table, but no matter how hard he glared, he had to admit they were right.

He slid beneath the surface of life like a crocodile in an algae-infested lake. No matter how hard he swam, no-one knew where he was.

His eyes widened and he tried to click his fingers several times before giving up. His 'Eureka' moments were never as dramatic as other people's. This was his strength; his anonymity was his disguise. He didn't need costumes and wigs and when he appeared he would be just like the crocodile. Actually, he didn't know what it was that a crocodile did, but it must be something effective- after all, they had to eat.

Percy sat hidden amongst the trees watching the new fort approach completion. *Yet another world-breaking scheme ended in ruin,* he thought.

The curse of the Plumm's had struck again. All his ancestors had been at the cusp of invention; they had supplied the inspiration for so many advances over the generations, but were they remembered? No! Was there a statue? No! The world was full of opportunists- that was the trouble. They would lurk around a genius like him and then pounce just as the idea was ready and claim it as their own.

He remembered the first time he was inspired. He was at school and the teacher asked them to 'invent something useful which would benefit mankind all over the world'.

Percy had licked his pencil and written furiously; the inspiration flowed. He devised a system where words and pictures could be sent into everyone's home to enrich and educate them. It involved invisible waves and a box in every home to catch them.

The teacher had snatched the paper away and sneered, "See this on *Television* by any chance, boy?" and walked away. Percy had never *seen* a television and yet when he left home, they were everywhere. He often wondered how much that teacher made out of it.

Percy sighed. Here he was again, the main provider to the Plumm clan and he had lost out again.

He brushed some of the glittery dust off his shoulder and wondered if he would ever succeed at anything.

Percy watched morosely as diggers swung around moving earth from one place to another. *Huh,* he thought, *pity they can't* throw *the stuff instead.* He sat up. "Why can't they?" he whispered to himself. "Surely with a bit of tinkering!" Percy liked tinkering.

Chapter Forty-Four

Cuthbert took a deep breath before he entered the attic. He had not been allowed in here until his parents both passed on and now there was no-one to stop him.

His father had always sucked in his breath, shook his head and said, "Cuthbert, you are a simple soul. You are one of the Valley's secrets and you should be kept from the world. If we let you loose in there, we wouldn't have a world to keep you from."

His mother had always turned pale and looked for his father.

Apart from borrowing a few props for the Shakespearean plays now and then, Cuthbert hadn't really had time to investigate.

The time had come. He pushed open the door.

Percy spent hours dismantling part of the back wall of his fort. When it was wide enough and no-one was looking, he crept out and stole the digger.

The rattling and clanking of its tracks was just part of the building sounds echoing from the hills, and he tucked it safely inside.

Using the adrenaline of success, he threw the wall back up and ran onto the walkway. "Hah! Hah!" he shouted, waving his fist. "Grass is nine tenths of the floor!"

One of the builders tapped his mate on the helmet and asked, "What does that twerp want?"

The other builder glanced up, shrugged and went back to his work, and then a thought occurred to him. "Didn't we have *two* diggers?"

The first builder sighed. "Flaming mafia, I'd better go down and see how much they want for it this time."

A nearby bush scratched its head.

Cuthbert moved some old sacking. This had been wrapped around the bows and arrows Geraldine used for one of the plays. He moved an empty box, then another. Then he looked inside an empty barrel. Everywhere he looked there were empty containers.

Had his father moved everything, or had he been burgled?

The security measures in this room were legendary; it would take someone either very brave or very stupid.

He moved closer to a huge bear-trap which had evidently been sprung; there was a hank of coarse red hair in the jaws.

"Percy!" he yelled.

Percy rubbed his hands with glee; he had a whole new shiny digger to play with. Black hydraulic hoses crawled all over it like veins on the arms of a strong-man. "Where are my spanners?" he breathed, dropping down the hole into the tunnel. He squeezed past the piles of weapons he had brought from Cuthbert's. He had enough crossbows to supply an army and those long pointy things would come in handy too. He found the spanners.

Marvin flipped through the pages in a frenzied state. He always appreciated the rules and regulations that bound the Local Authority together, until he needed to find something.

It seemed the Mayor was protected from everything barring fire explosion or collapse and it was almost impossible to remove him.

The labyrinth of planning rules was even worse; there were enough sub-clauses inserted in unlikely places to make one's eyes water.

He stayed calm as he replaced the book on the shelf; he was in the Local Authority's legal and accounts division office and normal rules did not apply in here. It was like a scene from Dickens, rows of desks manned by furtive little men, all scribbling into ledgers and conversing in hushed tones. This was the heart of the Local Authority. The heart-beat may be slow, but it resonated throughout the land.

It was best to tread carefully here. The only thing missing was the sight of goose quills and Marvin suspected a feather duster would have a low survival rate in here.

Thanking the librarian, Marvin walked the gauntlet of searching eyes. They watched him pass as if trying to define some clues as to what the outside world was really like.

Chapter Forty-Five

Percy was late for the meeting in Cuthbert's kitchen, but he swaggered in quite full of himself.

It was beginning to sink in that the Valley was lost and Geraldine snarled, "Wander in, why don't you? It's only all your fault, after all."

Percy took a seat and snapped, "At least I am preparing for battle and I've made a machine to sling rocks at their fort."

"*Trebuchet*," said Geraldine haughtily.

"*Gesundheit*," said Percy.

Henry as always called the meeting to order and made sure all sharp knives were locked away.

"It sounds as if Percy's right, actually; we are going to have to do battle for the Valley."

Ronald was never one to turn down a conflict, but he asked, "What difference will that make? Even if we beat them, they still own the Valley. We still need the deeds." He paused and added wolfishly, "Then we can thrash them just for fun."

All eyes turned towards Geraldine, who shrugged. "Neither Bogus, Sharp or Shifty admitted to holding the deeds. We can hardly search the whole office, can we?"

Even Elspeth's jaw dropped when she saw the size of the task. Margery was unusually quiet and Avril gibbered under her breath.

The file room seemed to stretch forever. There were boxes and ledgers stacked everywhere and every shelf was crammed with documents. The three women stood in their formal disguises of garishly flowered aprons and head cloths tied to make bunny ears on top of their heads.

Avril came to a decision and her bunny ears flopped about as she explained, "We don't need to check any documents older than three months, most of this lot relate to the Ark."

"Oh," said Elspeth, "if we find the deeds, we can also have our *own* theme park, complete with animals."

Margery's cloth ears flopped as she said cynically, "The way our luck is going, we would get a bill from the 'Ararat holdings Company' for back rent and end up bankrupt anyway."

All the other ears flopped forward solemnly as they all agreed.

"Besides," she added, "we only have a concrete lake and we can't even keep ourselves afloat, never mind an Ark."

The ears danced like daffodils in a poem and looked again at the daunting task before them.

A box file crashed to the floor from somewhere near Margery's ear and Jasper's face appeared in the gap. "Shifty is back in his office, they are all in the building now."

Margery thanked him and he disappeared. The women started searching for recently dated documents.

Elspeth reminded them it was actually a scroll they were looking for and they gazed around at a loss.

Avril wailed, "It could be anywhere and as a recent acquisition it is probably in a safe."

"Huh," said Elspeth mysteriously, "that would be *much* easier."

Percy had propped up a selection of crossbows on the walkway around his fort walls as the crow watched avidly, and then went back into the tunnel for arrows ... *bolts*!

Geraldine had made a meal of putting him straight in front of the others and explained that it was the origin of the expression 'A bolt from the blue.'

Percy had muttered darkly about 'A bolt next time *you* wear blue,' and then kept quiet.

Cuthbert had busied himself pouring red-hot tea for everyone from a huge teapot and was intent upon giving Percy more than a *verbal* scolding. Unfortunately, Percy seemed to have lots of itches and by the time Cuthbert could aim the kettle, Percy's hand was gone to scratch somewhere else, and the table in front of him was awash and the others were thirsty.

The crow hopped towards one of the contraptions the scruffy one had been fiddling with. The principle seemed simple enough. You put one foot in a metal bar and turned bright red trying to pull the string back until it latched and stayed where it was.

From his observations of Percy, the crow had deduced it was quite a boring job and random variations had been added. At the point where the scruffy one's face was as red as a winter berry, the string could snap.

This provided both relief and entertainment as the scruffy one threw down the offending article, screamed abuse and did a strange dance in those odd containers he kept his feet in.

The crow hopped onto the crossbow to work out what the end result would be after all this effort and balanced precariously in the 'V' shape where the string met the latch.

The thing had been left propped up pointing towards the sky and as far as the crow was concerned, it was just an ornament.

On the basic crow principle of if it won't move, peck it, the crow chipped down at the latch ... *everything became a blur!*

Margery and Avril were almost in tears. There was no end in sight to this job and they hadn't even started to find a dating system yet.

Right back where they had started from, Elspeth sat on a pile of papers and waved one at her friends in the distance. "I always said there was more to that Butcher than met the eye," she said. "Says here, he tried to buy the contract for taking bodies from Cuthbert's to the cemetery. Never did trust his meat pies."

The other two women turned back to their task, waving floppy ears at each other in acceptance of Elspeth's little eccentricities.

They spun back rapidly at a rasping sound from the far end where they had left their friend. Elspeth was briefly illuminated by a flame that stubbornly refused to light the match.

"What on earth are you doing, Elspeth?" cried Margery. "Put that out!"

Elspeth smiled. "What, after all that trouble I took to light it?"

Margery and Avril stared in horror as Elspeth- resembling a Halloween pumpkin- watched the keen yellow flame straining to become an inferno.

Elspeth spoke again. "It's all right, dears; I'll set fire to this end, you raise the alarm and we will see which scrolls they bother saving. Off you go!"

She moved her hand slightly and the flame flew up the shelves and across the piles of paper.

The two women went; their screams were better than any smoke detector.

The crow tumbled over and over inside the fort on the opposite side of the Valley, coming to rest against a builder's boot.

The builder stooped, picked it up and wiped his brow with it before throwing it down in disgust.

The crow dragged its dishevelled self under cover while it decided what had actually happened.

No-one questions the sight of two panic-stricken cleaning women screaming "Fire, fire!" as they run through a building, not even when one of them added as an afterthought "Save your valuable scrolls!"

The population of the building poured out into the street as smoke began to appear in the stairwells.

Secretaries carried handbags and juniors clutched electronic devices of all descriptions.

At last a man appeared with several back copies of the racing times and another one with a dartboard under his arm.

Margery and Avril waited. Mr Shifty scuttled out into the open with a *scroll* under his arm. "That's our man!" cried Margery delightedly. "Herd him towards the bushes."

Avril protested, "We'll never find him in there, Margery."

Margery ignored her and ran towards Shifty shouting, "Look out, the chimneys are falling!"

Shifty tensed and entered the bushes for cover. The bushes rustled in anticipation.

The crow had now been kicked, stepped on and wiped across several sweaty areas and had taken all he was going to take. He flapped up to the walkway and focused on the light reflecting from a helmet in Percy's fort.

Holding his wings at various angles, he sent a semaphore message across the gap to Percy, detailing how to calculate the range and angle of trajectory so as to land several arrows, sorry, bolts, in amongst the builders in sweet revenge.

Halfway through the instructions, the crow remembered who he was dealing with, but just sighed and carried on.

Percy was looking for the crow at that very moment; he needed a moving target.

A series of flickering movements from the other fort caught his eye and he rested one of Cuthbert's telescopes on the top of the fort wall.

There was the crow. *Make rude gestures at me, would you,* thought Percy, and fitted a bolt to a crossbow, the bow twanged and the bolt hummed across the gap, dropping short.

The crow was impressed; the scruffy one had hidden talents. He signalled adjustments to allow for a slight breeze and extra range and screwed up his eyes to watch the next bolt fly.

Much better, thought the crow, relishing his role as F.A.C. (Forward Air Crow) artillery.

The bolt hummed overhead and smacked into the back of a workman's helmet, which prompted him to hit the joker behind him with a shovel, and the fort soon resembled a Roman arena heaving with blood, sweat and testosterone.

The crow squawked with delight and drew his wing across his throat to signal 'cut' to stop Percy firing anymore.

Percy saw the gesture and scowled. *Cut my throat when you catch me, eh?* He ran along the walkway fitting bolts into all the crossbows and then kicked them in turn when he ran back.

The crow was appalled. He looked on as the sky darkened and a shower of bolts flew overhead whining past him one after the other to land inside the fort causing yelps and confusion.

The Cool brothers sheltered under the walkway and one of them observed, "It seems that the scruffy one is aware of our intentions, brother."

His brother agreed.

The crow shook his head. His instructions had been explicit; now Percy had given away his barrage capabilities.

Of course, he chided himself, it was partly his own fault. He forgot that the Valley had much thicker air than anywhere else he had flown. He also forgot that the Valley had never heard of metric measurements and on top of all that, he was dealing with an idiot. He flapped into the air and began to gain altitude, leaving the chaos behind him.

Percy rubbed his hands together "That made him take flight," he chuckled, and if anyone had been inside, it would have served them right for copying his fort.

Then he noticed they had made one change in his plans for a fort-they had fitted gates.

Those same gates now crashed open to disgorge a horde of angry builders, some with crossbow bolts sticking out of their hats. *And they were all coming his way.*

Elspeth came over to Margery and Avril. "Did it work?" she asked casually.

Margery studied her friend, calm, composed and collected, even under that smouldering headgear. "They will be discussing you everywhere now, dear," she said. "I can tell."

Elspeth frowned as she asked, "How?"

Margery smiled. "Your ears are on fire, dear."

Chapter Forty-Six

Jasper had already set up his stall outside the Mandrake Arms when the Valley met to celebrate. As potential customers arrived, he adjusted his baseball cap into 'relaxed, cheery-chap mode' and drawled, "Superb briefcase, ladies and gents, one careless owner, think about it, sir, take your time."

Cuthbert picked up a small square box and stood petrified as it shrieked eighty decibels of siren at him.

"Personal attack alarm," said Jasper smoothly. "Tested and working."

Henry admired a suit and Jasper winked at him. "Nice bit of stuff that, sir, seen action in all major court rooms, still warm."

Margery sidled up to Jasper and whispered "Make some pocket money later, Jasper. Where is the scroll?"

Jasper suddenly dived forward to demonstrate a shiny mobile phone to Avril, and Margery stepped after him. "The scroll, Jasper."

Seeing Jasper trying to sell the Captain a pair of socks, Margery felt a sudden chill.

"*Jasper*!" she screamed.

The scene froze into a tableau of market trader and guilty customers.

Jasper allowed his shoulders to slump and turned his cap backwards in an attempt to solicit sympathy. Removing the cap completely, Jasper began twisting it between his hands and took up a penitent stance before Margery. "You see, the truth is, well, what happened was …"

"Out with it," hissed Margery venomously.

Everyone stepped a pace back as the import of Margery's expression registered.

Jasper looked around vainly. "The truth is we've got a splinter faction," he mumbled.

"Who has?" asked Margery incredulously. "The Valley mafia?"

Jasper nodded miserably. "While we were asking Mr Shifty for donations for our market stall, some of the others made off with the scroll. They sent me a note saying that 'The Valley deeds are now in good hands, we could not trust the twerps who held them last'."

Margery stared at him in disbelief, and then was distracted as Percy went hurtling past chased by a gang of angry builders.

Turning to the other side, she watched Cuthbert trying to creep up on the attack alarm and take it by surprise.

"They may have a point," she conceded.

Margery sat with Jasper outside the Mandrake Arms. The rest went inside to celebrate anyway, just in case there was something to celebrate later.

Jasper had cleared his stall, but his heart hadn't been in it. His baseball cap never even reached the 'this is your lucky day' angle. Now he sat morosely, wondering whether he should hand over the reins of the mafia to someone else.

Margery had been tapping her fingernails against the wooden table top. She stopped, turned to Jasper and asked, "Wasn't that note rather too literate to have been written by the Valley mafia?"

Jasper pulled the peak of his hat down into 'thoughtful benefactor' mode and said, "Hmm."

Percy had evaded the builders by running up behind Blind-Pugh and leapfrogging over him so that when he turned and transformed into a black and white whirling dervish, there were only builders in reach.

Then he sneaked into the pub by the back way and joined Cuthbert. Percy was disappointed he had missed all the good stuff from Jasper's stall, especially when Cuthbert showed him the attack alarm. He planned to wait until it was asleep and then surprise it.

Cuthbert suddenly regarded his friend and asked why he ran from the builders when he had an impregnable fort to hide inside.

Percy couldn't think of a reply, so Cuthbert tried, "And why run all the way through the Valley when you could have slipped into the tunnel and ended up here anyway?"

After considering his reply carefully, Percy said, "So, it's an attack alarm, is it?"

The Cool brothers had received a late night visit from a man in his underwear claiming to be a solicitor.

141

One of the brothers thought he said 'soliciting' and called the Police, but Constable Beeching had been investigating a queue at the Pizza establishment and was unavailable.

Apparently, the mysterious stranger had developed an aversion to bushes and hidden in a rubbish skip for some time. This explained his fast food tray hat.

The other brother had tested the mysterious visitor to establish identity. When the man demanded a fee before the interview, they looked more closely and recognised Mr Shifty.

Anger is always a distorting emotion and one brother constantly referred back to why the solicitor had been in the bushes in his underwear in the first place?

The other brother saw the problem clearly indeed. *They no longer owned the Valley.*

Jasper wandered amongst his troops. The new Cinema building didn't get much use after Percy offered to maintain the projectors and the mafia had appropriated one of the storerooms as a headquarters.

They were engaged in the routine maintenance pastimes recognised by most youths of their age.

There was catapult elastic to replace, pen knives to oil and that panic-stricken solicitor had caused quite a bit of damage to the lightweight summer issue bushes.

Several lads were dispatched for more foliage and Clive had returned already with some early daffodils.

Jasper studied the faces around him. In the confusion one bush had looked much like another and he did not know who had taken the scroll. No-one seemed nervous and no-one showed signs of wealth.

A greenish gleam flashed in one of the dark corners, but Jasper ignored it. He was busy studying faces. No-one was sweating and the banter seemed normal for apprentice criminal organisations everywhere.

The green glow appeared again briefly and Jasper wandered over to the dark corner where they developed their surveillance photos.

Egbert was busy washing the negatives in chemicals and the green glow came from his wrist when he pulled them out of the tray.

Jasper thought hard.

Egbert was a long standing mafia member, but didn't take part in field-work. Several operations had been aborted, because he owned a Mickey Mouse watch and Mickey only had one hand. Neither Mickey nor Egbert landed in the place they were supposed to be at the time the others did.

"Anyone got the time?" Jasper asked, innocently.

Egbert's wrist flashed and he replied instantly. He was wearing a military issue watch with green luminous fingers. There was no sign of the 'armless mouse'.

"New watch, Egbert?" asked Jasper, moving closer.

"Yes, thanks, Jasper, it was just what I needed."

"Who gave it to you?" asked Jasper, suspicion beginning to dawn.

Egbert paused with a photo mid-way to the tray. "One of the other bushes," he replied with a frown. "I assumed it was you."

Jasper stayed expressionless as he asked, "The scroll?"

Egbert frowned again. "I thought you held it for me when I tried the watch on, then we all came back."

Jasper patted his comrade on the shoulder and moved away. Who else did they know who roamed disguised as shrubbery and would have a military watch spare?

"Ronald!" he hissed.

Ronald sat before a roaring log fire in the lounge of the Mandrake Arms; he smiled into the flames and sipped his drink.

It had always been his habit to celebrate success with a brandy. There hadn't been too much of that lately.

The heat from the brandy worked on him from the inside and the log fire warmed his face.

Ronald smiled a secret smile again as he thought of himself as a landowner. The smile grew wider as he imagined being Cuthbert and Percy's landlord.

He dozed for a moment until a slight scuffling sound caused him to open one eye. *Old building, mice behind the wainscoting,* he thought. The lights dimmed. *Old* wiring, mice in the ceiling, he thought as he dozed once more. His arms seemed heavy and his armchair vibrated slightly. *Old chair, mice in the upholstery,* he speculated.

A clatter came from up the chimney and smoke billowed into the room. Ronald's eyes flashed open. *That's not mice,* his instincts told him. "Rats! It's the Valley mafia," he muttered as he realised they had taped him into his chair.

Two members of the Valley mafia dropped down from the huge inglenook fireplace. They crouched each side like soot-blackened fire-dogs as Ronald struggled against his bonds.

Another member appeared beside him with a bag of marshmallows. Jasper came into his vision.

Everyone watched everyone else as one of the youths began to toast the marshmallows on a stick; the smell began to fill the room.

Ronald adopted the hard-man mercenary stance and sneered, "Think I haven't been threatened before; what can you lot do to me that half the armies of the world have failed at?"

He glared at his captors as Jasper dropped a newly roasted marshmallow onto Ronald's knee and watched it sizzle.

Margery entered the lounge on her circuit, checking doors and windows for the night. She didn't lock, to save the Valley mafia breaking anything as they passed through.

She stopped in front of the subdued figure of a trussed Ronald. Cocking her head to one side, she studied him. He was firmly taped into the old armchair and parts of his anatomy still smoked.

He was asleep now and still breathing, so the boys must have got what they wanted.

Margery patted his cheek and said, "Goodnight, Ronald, good of you to amuse the children," and left him there.

Percy prodded Ronald's laptop suspiciously.

Cuthbert caught him shaking it yesterday. He had been watching football and wanted to see if "all the little men would fall out." Now he watched an aerial view of something; it looked like a load of ramshackle buildings, and one of them had smoke coming out of its chimney.

Percy fiddled with some knobs and tapped some keys and a voice came out of the speakers.

"Well, as far as I'm concerned, *they* haven't got the deeds either, so if we attack quickly, take the nincompoops' fort and claim the village, we will have possession on our side. We can then close off the Valley and do as we like."

"Is that the Cool brothers?" asked Cuthbert.

Percy shrugged and started to close the lid.

"Probably some TV programme," he said. "They all look the same to me."

Cuthbert stood beside him. "What do you mean?"

They both stared at the screen as Percy explained. "It's like when you watch a regular series and they suddenly introduce a new character. He gets killed so that the original cast survive. Have you ever noticed that everyone drives a brand new car and as soon as an older model appears, that's the one which is going to crash?"

Cuthbert looked puzzled. "What's that got to do with what you're watching?"

Percy sighed. "Look at that dump; they've made it especially so that it can be burnt down in a dramatic fashion after the escaped lunatics take it over and murder everyone."

Cuthbert swallowed. "Do you watch *much* TV, Percy?"

Percy shrugged. "Used to, before gardening took up all my time. There! What did I tell you? Someone's coming. Look!"

Sure enough, two figures were approaching the buildings. "Those two will have escaped from the asylum, the people in the house will be murdered and someone else will come to ask directions from the two nutcases. A lamp will be knocked over and the place will burn down with the hero just crawling to safety."

The first two men were almost at the house when another figure appeared some distance behind them.

"There," said Percy pointing, "that's the hero.

"He walks just like a penguin," noted Cuthbert.

Percy warned that the tension would have to build up, so something would delay the first two outside and, sure enough, one of them seemed to stumble and start hopping about just to prove he really was a lunatic. The two men then disappeared below the eaves of the house.

Cuthbert chewed his knuckles and almost took his fingers off when the door flew open and Henry announced, "You really must clear your yard up, Cuthbert. The Captain has got his foot stuck in a bucket … what's that you're watching?"

Cuthbert explained about the plot and predicted the flames any minute now. "The whole dump is going to go up," he said excitedly.

"Isn't that your dump?" asked Ronald as he entered behind the others.

The room fell silent.

"Percy!" exploded Ronald. "I told you never to touch that. You've managed to reverse the surveillance and transmit everything back to the Cool brothers. Do they know about the microphone in the model, the lost deeds and everything?"

"*We do now!*" said a voice from the speaker.

Ronald slammed the lid down on the fingers of his other hand and ran outside. Sure enough, there was a model plane circling overhead filming them from above. Ronald shook his fists impotently, but Percy had spotted the crow.

He held out an arm and gave a piercing whistle. The crow flapped in from somewhere and settled heavily on Percy's arm.

"There! You see it, my beauty? There is your prey; fly, *fly my beauty, fly!*"

The assembly was duly impressed by this 'Boris Karloff' moment, but the crow had assumed a piece of chocolate was on offer and blunted his beak trying to get Percy's helmet off.

Percy ran around in circles trying to shake the crow into flight, even flapping his own arms until they almost took off in tandem.

The crow gave up the search and finally looked skywards. His eyes and beak widened; he had seen one of those things before and they bit.

He looked Percy squarely in the eye and thought, *I might have a hump on my back, mate, but that doesn't make me a Sopwith Camel,* and bit Percy's nose.

The two of them ended up rolling around the farmyard in a swirl of straw and feathers, whilst the others rolled their eyes and walked away from this primitive, on-going struggle between man and nature.

Chapter Forty-Seven

With a sticking plaster on his nose, Percy sat at Elspeth's kitchen table waiting to lick the bowl.

Elspeth and Margery had mixed some of the strangest ingredients Percy had ever seen and when he licked the spoon, his lips had turned green.

The two women were thoroughly absorbed as they worked and conversation was at a minimum- this was always a problem for Percy. Just as nature abhors a vacuum, Percy hates a void. He found silence offensive on several levels and made it his duty to combat such evils.

"It's funny that you two should be making that stuff," he began. "One of my ancestors invented 'Egyptian Flames' and it saved the day at some great sea battle."

"Do you mean 'Greek Fire'?" asked Elspeth vaguely as she poured a mixture into empty bottles.

"That was Archimedes, wasn't it, dear?" asked Margery, equally busy, moulding exploding pastry into regular shapes. "They fired it at the ship's sails and lifted the siege?"

"I believe you are right, dear," allowed Elspeth as she banged a cork into a bottle.

Percy sat up. "Did I say Egyptian? Dear me, no! I meant 'Irish Fire', different altogether. Anyway, my ancestor ..."

"That brings back memories. *Irish Fire*, remember that, Margery?"

Margery nodded. "Oh, yes, that involved whiskey, didn't it?"

Percy cleared his throat. "Anyway, when my ancestor invented 'Russian Fire' he ..."

Elspeth threw her head back and laughed. "I'd forgotten about that one; vodka wasn't it, dear?"

Margery shook her head in wonder. "How could we forget that one? What a night!"

Percy glowered. "Now I remember," he said firmly, "it was 'Spanish Fire' and he ..."

The two women came each to a side and picked up the chair with Percy still in it and held him in mid-air. Elspeth placed something under the legs on one side and Margery stuck something under the legs on the other side.

Percy looked from one to the other as they counted "One-two-three!" and dropped him.

All four legs exploded at once and the legs were immediately shortened by three inches.

Percy looked up at the two women and glared. "Still want to lick the bowl, Percy?" asked Elspeth.

Going for relaxed and casual, Percy put his feet up on the table above him and his hands behind his head. "Don't mind if I do, ladies."

The stream of gold dust pouring out of his welly into a glittering cone on the floor attracted everyone's eye.

Now Percy heard a *real* silence.

Chapter Forty-Eight

Ronald, Henry, the Captain and Cuthbert sat around the table in Cuthbert's kitchen.

The mood was not good. Ronald had only a small amount of explosives left and had been trying to sell the idea of a suicide bomber to destroy the other fort. *He* couldn't do it, of course, because he had to master-mind all subsequent attempts should that one be a success.

Henry explained he had absolutely no sense of direction; he could end up anywhere.

The Captain actually laughed out loud. "With my back?" he said in horror. "It would be *murder!*"

Cuthbert stirred his tea morosely until some latent sense told him that he was being watched. He looked into each of his companions faces in turn, thought carefully and said, "Pardon?"

The kitchen door burst open and Margery and Elspeth stormed in carrying Percy between them. They slammed him down into a chair and stood each side of him glaring furiously as they regained their normal breathing rate.

Cuthbert was relieved, as Ronald had been holding up this waistcoat full of pockets for him to try on. Cuthbert always avoided anything with loads of useful pockets; by the time he found the vital gadget, the emergency was usually over.

Percy gave everyone a sickly smile, raised both of his hands and pleaded, "I was going to tell you."

"*When?*" snapped both women in stereo.

"What on earth is going on?" asked Henry, looking at his wife.

In reply, Margery and Elspeth held perfumed handkerchiefs to their noses and forcibly removed Percy's welly; tipping it up on the table, they made another glittering cone of gold dust.

"I was going to tell you," insisted Percy desperately.

"*When*, after we had asked you where all your new stuff came from?" snarled Ronald.

Percy folded under all the withering looks and explained about the old mine and the miners and the flooded cellar and the gold. Somehow, he didn't come out of it as the hero.

After staring at the pile of dust silently for a while, Henry said, "We could buy the Valley back."

The Captain said, "We could buy loads of weapons."

Ronald said, "We could buy a tank."

Margery said, "We could instruct solicitors to keep the deeds safe in future. I know a firm who work cheap and they need new offices; in fact they're working out of a tent."

Cuthbert said, "Pardon?"

Percy looked around wildly. No-one was looking at him, but they were certainly discussing him.

Ronald fitted him with some sort of waistcoat and Margery opened a box of pastry and put several items in his pockets.

The Captain muttered about a 'suicide vest' and Henry suggested 'remote control'.

Every now and then one of them would look at Percy and shake their heads sadly.

Margery filled his last pocket and Elspeth stuck a wire from his helmet into his collar.

They all stepped back, someone opened the door and Henry said, "Off you go, Percy, there's a good chap."

Percy gave one last panic-stricken look around and ran off wailing into the night.

Someone closed the door and Ronald asked Margery, "What did you put in his pockets?"

Margery smirked at them and replied mischievously, "Three rock cakes, seven scones and a jam tart."

Percy's moods seemed to fluctuate as he got older. First he was sad that his friends had sent him off to blow himself up; then he was happy when the wire fell off his helmet and the vest didn't go off. Then he was miserable that it took him hours to pluck up the courage to empty one of the pockets. Then he was happy that it was *real* pastry, because he had been hungry. Then he was angry because he had been tricked and he had missed dinner.

"Perhaps I'm going through the change?" he asked himself, and then shrugged. "As long as I don't change into Cuthbert, I should be all right."

Playing with a pile of gold dust had soon become boring. Solid gold cutlery was one thing and gold watches definitely another, but a handful of suspect glittery bits soon lost its allure.

More tea was served and Cuthbert went out to milk a goat, but the bottle he came back with looked suspiciously like something from a shop.

Nobody asked; life was too short.

Percy came back into the kitchen as if he was a land owner back from checking his boundaries and discovering that he didn't have any.

He laid a poster on the table and proceeded to fill all his new pockets with tea, sugar, biscuits and coffee in case they chased him out again.

Henry read the poster. "'First of its kind. Open-air Sledgehammer battle to celebrate the first stage of the creation of Sledgehammer World. Join the invaders and help to clear the natives from the site and then help us to colonise the Valley. Costumes must be of an approved type, bought at an approved price from an approved Sledgehammer shop.'"

Percy was aghast. "That's not fair," he wailed. "They said I had the helmet concession!" His voice trailed off as people began to realise he was there.

Henry squinted at something and read, "'Apply for tickets at www.sledgeworld.com.'"

Ronald enquired, "So, they've admitted it's a 'dot-con' then?"

Chapter Forty-Nine

The Cool brothers stood amongst the wreckage of the scale model of the site gazing in awe at the tapestry.

They had smashed the wonderful model to pieces trying to find the microphone, until one of them simply lifted the top off a mountain.

"It has all come to pass," said one of them reverently as they opened invisible safes in homage to the dragon dropping from heaven on the wall.

"The idiots haven't found the one behind the tapestry yet, Elspeth!" crowed Ronald, hunched over his laptop.

Elspeth gave a little smile of a job well done. *You've still got it girl*, she thought.

The computers crashed around mid-day, the telephone lines melted and the social sites became downright hostile.

Queues stretched for miles in any town with a Sledgehammer concession shelf tucked away somewhere in its cellar.

The Cool brothers referred to this as 'Dungeon-Selling' and the retailers called it 'embarrassment.'

Tickets were the new 'must-have' for a certain disassociated tribe of loosely affiliated geeks, who seemed to be able to conjure up funds out of nowhere whenever 'Sledgehammer' was involved.

Costumes had been carefully hoarded and customised from past Halloweens and several belts and neck-chains carried dolls-heads stolen from screaming sisters over the years.

The mood and the crowd were both turning ugly.

Percy paced up and down; he thought he was alone in his fort until a clonking on his helmet reminded him of the crow on his shoulder.

He rehearsed his 'eve of battle' speech a bit pointlessly really, with only a crow to inspire. He carried on pacing, trying to remember excerpts from famous examples.

"And all those people still abed will soon be stomping Percy instead."

That didn't sound very inspiring, so he tried, "If the enemy wish to die, then we shall accommodate them, be ferocious in war but magnanimous in victory!"

With only two of them defending the fort, Percy wondered which of those options sounded the least painful. He shook his head; it was hard to put a positive spin on this one.

He climbed up to the walkway and surveyed the Valley. All the crossbows were lined up and loaded and he had trained the crow to run along them pecking the string when he cried "volley fire."

Lots of sharp pointy spears lined up also, and he had opened a box of leather slings. He heard these could be deadly long range, but after hours of practice, knew only the chap behind him would be in trouble.

He had no trouble spotting the enemy though; they had been arriving for hours. For some reason, they preferred to travel in blunt-nosed motor caravans with roofs that popped up like a striped concertina every time they hit a bump; it was like being invaded by ice-cream vans.

One particular chap seemed to be stirring everyone up; he had long hair blowing across his face and his knees jerked rhythmically as he rabble-roused. He held a long red and white striped pole with a dolls head on it.

Percy levelled his telescope and recognised Winston, who apparently had a shaman as his alter-ego. Percy looked around his empty fort and gulped.

The new cinema building was bustling. The miners had been invited to join the residents and Cuthbert threw open the chests of theatre props and deceased effects.

The Captain paraded in a black suit far too small for him, wearing a top hat with its crown flapping. Patches of bare white skin showing at wrist and ankles made him look like a skeleton dressed for a students' ball. "If I'm going out, I'm going out in style!" he announced ironically.

Ronald was decked out in a black assault suit with bulging pockets and Elspeth explained the finer points of an exploding sausage roll.

The miners left after a brief whispered conversation with Henry and everyone assumed they were leaving the Valley to it, but the handshake as they parted said differently.

A sudden silence fell upon the hall as Margery entered. Her hair fell across her shoulders and she had draped an old fur coat across them as a long cloak; she was a convincing warrior queen men would be prepared to die for.

She surveyed the assembly and everyone strained to hear her words.

"You don't have to follow me," she began quietly, "but if it is our lot to lose the Valley to a pile of Dragon Droppings, *we* will make that decision. *To War!*" she roared and led the way out of the cinema.

Chapter Fifty

Percy tried to loosen his collar as the enemy massed on the other side of the Valley.

Shouts were heard and wooden staffs banged upon dustbin lid shields; the mass of invaders began to move forward.

The crow tapped urgently onto Percy's helmet, directing him to point his telescope at the village. People swarmed out of the cinema, and they were in costume.

Percy jumped up and down in excitement, but stopped as they all streamed into the pub.

"Oh!" he said.

He sat disconsolately on the walkway with his little legs dangling over the edge. The crow squawked and tapped on his helmet.

Percy muttered, "I know, I know, there are thousands of them and they would be at the gates if we had gates."

The crow kept hammering away. Looking up in desperation, Percy saw people coming up out of the hole and into his fort.

Of course, he thought, *that's why they headed for the pub, to use the tunnel.*

He stood erect and cleared his throat; this was the moment for his eve of battle speech.

Margery looked magnificent. She pointed over the back wall and yelled, "Ladies, over the wall, you know what to do, we will attack by stealth and guile!"

Damn, thought Percy, *I could have used that.*

He opened his mouth again as a 'dancing skeleton' shouted, "Once more into the breach, dear friends, fear not the slings and arrows of adversity!"

Percy glared. He could have used that too! He tried to shout and rally his troops, as Elspeth screamed, "Flutter your lashes and go for the soft bits!"

Percy gave up and muttered "hell-fire" the excited crow mistook for "volley-fire" and released a barrage of crossbow bolts towards the other fort.

He looked over the parapet.

The screaming hordes were coming straight at them when they suddenly found a barricade of crossbow bolts had erected a fence right across their path. The other side of the barrier was suddenly filled with comely wenches carrying trays of pastries and handing out free samples.

One of the Cool brothers screamed, "Approved Sledgehammer snacks only!" at the top of his voice from the other fort.

The other one yelled, "What the devil are those bushes doing?"

The Valley mafia closed in from both sides in a classic am-bush.

The enemy front rank stood around sampling the pastry and the ones at the back saw the trays empty rapidly.

Geraldine had taken charge of the converted digger and Henry was at the controls. Plastic-bottle bombs were flung in a scattering arc across the Valley floor and the enemy assumed they were soft drinks to complement the free pastries.

Sensing a turn in the tide of battle, Margery screamed, "Why didn't you put gates in, Percy, you clown?" She then added, "Thank you, dear" as Arkle smashed a hole for them to charge through.

"*Trebuchet*!" yelled Geraldine every time she had reloaded the bucket.

"*Gesundheit*!" shouted Percy in return.

The Valley filled with explosions as pastries and bottles went off, the mafia bushes forced a wedge through the middle of the mass and started fighting outwards from there.

Percy threw spears as if his life depended upon it. Eventually, Ronald pointed him in the right direction because *their* lives depended upon it.

The Cool brothers just gaped. They outnumbered this rabble, whoever they were. And besides, it was only supposed to be the scruffy one in the fort.

Someone handed one of the brothers a meat pasty and he absently lifted it to his mouth. His brother knocked it out of his hand saying, "Official food only," and they both stared as it lay there *hissing*.

They turned to each other. "How?" they asked as an arrow-shaped crow screamed past in-between them.

Suddenly, their fort was being surrounded by an angry enemy force. Their own troops returned to complain that, "These helmets don't keep arrows out and now we can't get them off, oh, I'm bleeding," and "I can't stand here all day, I've got a school to run, have we won yet?"

One of the Cool brothers was accosted by someone who lost several teeth to the exploding pastry. "I told you, *official Sledgehammer snacks only!*" he snapped, forcing his way past.

The tide had really turned and the mass of invaders now hammered against the Cool brothers' fort, bottle bombs exploded overhead and everyone demanded entry to shelter from them.

The Cool brothers watched in horror as their Dragon Dropping flag lowered in a signal of surrender, before disappearing down the new tunnel dug by the miners. The crowds tore open the gates and stepped back as their own men streamed inside in panic.

They surveyed the battlefield.

It was like the aftermath of Waterloo.

A huge apparition in tweeds stood in a cleared space with unconscious bodies radiating out from her.

Several bushes went through the pockets of the fallen and a chap in black overalls made a necklace from all the dolls' heads he salvaged.

The brothers sleepwalked amongst the detritus of battle. "It's as if they had help from supernatural forces," said a stunned Cool brother.

Suddenly, the earth heaved before them and a terrible stench assailed their nostrils.

A creature loomed from the very ground dripping and emitting a terrifying wheezing sound. Another one appeared beside the first and its evil eye swivelled alarmingly; the third figure was huge and they stood dripping like foul mud-monsters from the depths of hell.

"Sorry about that," said the drains inspector, appearing behind his team. "We took a wrong turn and followed the sewers."

The Cool brothers had fainted clean away.

With everyone gone, the Valley looked like an exploded joke shop; wigs, vampire teeth, dolls' heads, bent plastic swords and rubber masks littered the floor.

The only living being still around from the enemy side was Winston. Nailed to the wall of Percy's fort by his coat with his red and white pole shoved through his sleeves, presumably still pledging his allegiance, he was muttering, "Cool! Cool!"

Chapter Fifty-One

Cuthbert's kitchen was a place of goodwill and best wishes. The Valley had once again fought off everything the real world and Percy could throw at them.

Piping mugs of tea were handed outside to the road gang, and the miners were toasted for their success with the early surrender.

"While you are here, gentlemen," said Henry, "what do you make of this?"

He tipped Percy's gold dust onto the table and the men laughed. "Oh, we know all about that," they said. "That's the fool's gold we found and smashed it into dust, so it wouldn't be mistaken for the real thing. We found that when digging near the pub, I'm afraid. That's why your cellar leaked in the first place, sorry, ma'am." They addressed this to Margery at the head of the table, who smiled beneficently as if she could have them beheaded later if she felt like it.

Just then, the door opened and Cuthbert staggered in, covered in scratches, bruises and with a glowing black eye. He stumbled to a chair and everyone gathered around him.

"Good heavens, man," said the Captain. "You look as if you fought them off alone."

Henry asked, "Did we leave you on the field, Cuthbert? We never even saw you."

Cuthbert waved down the praise modestly. "It was nothing," he gasped. "We all played our part."

"Ahem!" said the pot-plant in the corner.

"Anyone would have done the same," insisted Cuthbert nervously.

"*AHEM!*" insisted the pot-plant.

Cuthbert spluttered, "Heat of battle, confused images, no more than anyone else, you know."

"*Cuthbert!*" roared the pot-plant.

"*Oh, all right,*" said Cuthbert furiously. "I went to fetch Avril so that she could do a 'Local man saves Valley single-handed' feature and I took her through the tunnels. Unfortunately, she had one of those spiral note-books again and caught me staring at it in the dark."

"She did all that?" roared Ronald, pointing to Cuthbert's injuries. "Why did she stop before she killed you?"

Cuthbert glanced at everyone in turn and admitted, "I used my attack alarm."

"Did she get the story then, Cuthbert?" asked a smirking Margery.

Cuthbert slumped. "No, she thought it was all a trick and went back."

"*Thank you!*" said Jasper.

Percy rubbed his hands together as he waited for his guests to arrive.

Margery had loaned him the big room over the Mandrake Arms and he had salvaged the huge model from the Cool brother's office.

He had rebuilt it as a damaged Sledgehammer war site and his men lurked in shadowy recesses and waited on hidden pathways for the enemy to assemble.

The door opened and his adversaries began to file in led by Winston twitching to the neurological beat. His knee-caps were causing utter confusion to those following him up the stairs.

Percy contained his glee as rucksacks were parked in a corner and special compartmented boxes were opened to reveal the rival armies.

Not a word was spoken as the players bent over their task, fringes swinging like Aberdeen Angus cattle at a trough.

Percy stepped forward and placed his newest army in position. His men gleamed, every sword shone and every breast-plate blazed.

He stared through a magnifying lens for so long, as he painted them, that one eye was now bigger than the other.

"Let the games begin!" he announced and then turned to his own bag for his dice and the special tape measures and rule cards.

When he turned back to the battle-board, he gaped; it was covered in tanks! Ugly brutish things with long guns and nasty clanking tracks. The long-haired one swept a load of Percy's men off the table as he shouted "Bang!"

The other long-haired one swept the rest off the other side with another "Bang!" and the last long-haired one simply drove his tank right over Percy's hidden troops crunching their little bows and swords under the tracks.

"What, what, *what?*" screamed Percy.

Winston gestured a hand across the remnants of Percy's immaculate army. "Sledgehammer's old news, dude," he said. "We've gone *nuclear*," and he tipped the table over.

159

Henry looked upwards. *Right on time, Percy,* he thought as a door slammed upstairs. He ran to open the front door. *I knew it would end in tears.*

Percy stamped out of the pub, his hard work ruined.

All those hours painting moustaches onto little faces and putting bronze tips on all the arrow-heads; all wasted!

Every little man pasteurised by one big bomb. He had salvaged the dragon tapestry too and hung it in his shed, but the roof leaked, and now it was the Great Dragon Dripping!

There must be something he could win at.

Where was that crow?

~ The End ~

About the Author

Patrick Barrett is a sixty year old ex-miner from Mansfield in Nottinghamshire. He is married to Paula and between them, they have several children. 'Shakespeare's Cuthbert' was his first book, though he has been writing comedy for several years.

His aims as a writer are 'to be successful and make people laugh by providing them with an escape from the harshness of real life'.

His other abiding interest is in antiques.

www.ingramcontent.com/pod-product-compliance
Lightning Source LLC
Chambersburg PA
CBHW051302250626
47155CB00009B/3394